D0031508

the DReaM BEareR

ALSO BY WALTER DEAN MYERS

Fiction

Crystal

Handbook for Boys

It Ain't All for Nothin'

Monster
2000 Michael L. Printz Award
1999 Coretta Scott King Author Honor Book
1999 National Book Award Finalist

The Mouse Rap

Patrol

The Righteous Revenge of Artemis Bonner

Scorpions
A 1989 Newbery Honor Book

The Story of the Three Kingdoms

Nonfiction

Angel to Angel: A Mother's Gift of Love

Bad Boy: A Memoir

Brown Angels: An Album of Pictures and Verse

Malcolm X: A Fire Burning Brightly

Now Is Your Time! The African-American Struggle for Freedom
1992 Coretta Scott King Author Award

Awards

1994 ALA Margaret A. Edwards Award for lifetime achievement in writing for young adults

1994 ALAN Award for outstanding contribution to the field of young adult literature

WALTER DEAN MYERS

the DReaM BEareR

HarperCollins*Publishers*

Amistad

The Dream Bearer
Copyright © 2003 by Walter Dean Myers
All rights reserved. No part of this book may be used or reproduced
in any manner whatsoever without written permission except in the
case of brief quotations embodied in critical articles and reviews.
Printed in the United States of America. For information address
HarperCollins Children's Books, a division of HarperCollins
Publishers, 1350 Avenue of the Americas, New York, NY 10019.
www.harperchildrens.com
Library of Congress Cataloging-in-Publication Data
Myers, Walter Dean, date.
  The dream bearer / Walter Dean Myers. — 1st ed.
    p. cm.
  Summary: During a summer in Harlem, David relies on his
mother and a close friend and on an old man he meets in the park
to help him come to terms with his father's outbursts and unstable
behavior.
  ISBN 0-06-029521-X — ISBN 0-06-029522-8 (lib. bdg.)
  1. African Americans—Juvenile fiction. [1. African Americans—
Fiction. 2. Fathers and sons—Fiction. 3.Family life—New York
(State)—New York—Fiction. 4. Harlem (New York, N.Y.)—
Fiction.] I. Title.
PZ7.M992 Dr 2003   2002012878
[Fic]—dc21   CIP
                                                                AC

Typography by Karin Paprocki
    2   3   4   5   6   7   8   9   10
❖
First Edition

FOR MIRIAM, MY BUDDY

tHe DReaM BEareR

"So why are you building a house up here on the roof?"

"To show I can do it," Sessi said. "This is the way my ancestors in Kenya built their houses."

Loren and I watched as Sessi folded strips of dried palm leaves and wove them through the sticks she had made into a four-foot wall. She did look like she knew what she was doing.

"How many people can you get into one of these little houses?" Loren asked.

"This is just a model, silly," Sessi said. "If I were in my country, all of my family would help build the house and it would be ten times this big."

"They don't have to pay rent, right?" I asked.

"If you live on somebody else's lands, then you have

to pay rent," Sessi said.

"If I was in your little country, I would probably be a king or something," Loren said. "At least the mayor."

Sessi, on her knees, turned her head sideways and looked up at Loren. "Tarzan told you that?"

"He didn't have to," Loren said. "I just know it."

"I'm thinking of going to Africa when I get old enough," I said. "Just to check it out."

"Me and David are American." Loren nudged me with his elbow. "But we're part African."

"Who are you? Ibo? Edo?" Sessi asked. "All you guys are is American. I am Kikuyu."

"Yo, David, when she finishes making her house, you want to come up here and tear it down?" Loren put one hand on the house and pushed it gently.

"That's what Americans do," Sessi said, turning back to her model house. "You tear things down."

"Nothing wrong with that," Loren said.

Sessi made a little noise with her throat and shook her head. That was the thing with Sessi—sometimes she would make little noises that sounded almost like words or move her hands in a way that was almost like talking. She was pretty, with a smile that started with her mouth and spread across her face in a way that always made me smile when I saw it.

Loren was the same age as me, twelve, and lived in my building. Sessi lived in the building next to mine.

When the weather wasn't too bad, we sometimes went over the rooftops to get to each other's houses. Sessi wasn't like most girls I knew—she never put anybody down or got into arguments. Maybe it was because she was African, I didn't know.

"We could use your model house for our clubhouse," I said to Sessi. "You know what a clubhouse is?"

"I've been in this country for four years and I'm only one year younger than you are, Mr. David Curry," Sessi said. When she stood up she was an inch taller than me even though she was younger. "*Whatever* you boys know, I know."

"Oh, yeah? Why did the moron throw an alarm clock out the window?" Loren asked.

"Don't ask me silly things," Sessi said, rolling her eyes in Loren's general direction. "Do I look like a silly person to you?"

"Because he wanted to see time fly!" Loren said. "Get it? He wanted to see time fly!"

"Loren, that is so stupid!" Sessi went back to building her model house.

"The only reason you're smart is because your mother makes you study and stuff," Loren said. "If me and David studied all the time, we'd be twice as smart as you. Ain't that right, David?"

"I don't know," I answered.

"I'd think we'd be twice as smart as anybody if

we tried," Loren said.

"What do you think of us using it as a clubhouse?" I asked again.

"I'll have to ask my father," Sessi said. "I don't think he'll mind, but he'll have to be asked."

"When are you going to ask him?"

"When he gets home from work." Sessi smoothed the side of her house with the palm of her hand. "Maybe after supper."

"What's your dumb brother Kimi doing?" Loren asked.

"Reading to my mother," Sessi answered. "He's helping her with the citizenship test. She can read well, but it helps her to hear the words read aloud."

"You know you can't become a citizen without my permission," Loren said.

"Loren Hart, shut up!" Sessi spoke with finality.

"I don't know anybody with a real clubhouse," I said. "You think your father's going to say we can use it?"

"Tell him he'd better say yes or I might have to come to your house and deal with him!" Loren said.

"You're going to deal with my father?" Sessi held up her thumb and put it on the end of Loren's nose. "I don't think so!"

Loren gave her a look, but he didn't say anything and I knew he wasn't sure if he could beat Sessi or not. He had told me before that he thought Africans were tougher than they looked.

"I got to go home." Loren wiped his hands on the front of his jeans. "You want to come to my house and watch television?"

"I can't stay out too long," I said. "Mom's going to some kind of meeting, and she wants me home when she leaves."

"David's a good boy," Sessi said. "He listens to his parents."

"I think you want to marry him," Loren said. "If I go downstairs right now, I'll bet you'll be giving him a kiss before I get to the third floor."

"*Child*," Sessi said to Loren. "You're a mere child."

"I'll come over for a while," I said.

"Why don't you check with your mother first?" Sessi looked up at me. "Then if you go you'll have an easy mind."

"Yeah, I guess."

Loren pretended he was going to push Sessi's house down again and grinned as she balled up her fist and shook it at him.

We said good-bye to Sessi, went to our roof, and started through the door that led from the roof to the stairwell.

On the stairs Loren said he thought the little building on the roof was too small to be a clubhouse, that we wouldn't be able to do anything in it.

"It'll just be a place to hang out," I said. "A place to

go sometime if we don't feel like going downstairs."

"As long as Sessi doesn't want to be there all the time," Loren said.

"Sessi's okay," I said.

"Would you have her for a girlfriend?" Loren asked.

"I guess. You?"

"I guess."

I got home and found out that the meeting wasn't until eight. Mom said it would be okay for me to go to Loren's house for a while.

"Make sure you're home for supper," she said. "And don't you and Loren give Mrs. Hart a hard time."

"Is he home?" I asked, lowering my voice.

"You mean your brother?" Mom asked, knowing I didn't mean Tyrone. I meant Reuben.

"No."

"He's working," she said, glancing at the clock over the oven. "Why don't you go on before he comes home."

"Okay."

"Have fun with Loren," she added.

Loren Hart has been my best friend for as long as I can remember. I don't even remember how we became best friends. We just started hanging out when we were in the third grade and kept on doing it. He's smart, but he likes to act dumb and say dumb things. I like him to do that too, because sometimes he's really funny. He's light-skinned—I guess because his mother is white—

and kind of nice-looking. A girl in our old school said that he was too pretty to be a boy.

The thing I like about Loren most is that if you do something good or do something bad, it doesn't make a difference to him, he's always the same. Also he told me once, when we were coming home from a movie, that I was the best friend he had ever had. That meant a lot to me.

When I got to his house, Loren was watching cartoons. We watched them for almost an hour, but I was already thinking about Reuben.

I woke up in the middle of the night and heard the angry voices through the door. I got up on one elbow and listened to see if I could figure out what was going on. Mom's voice was high, and she was talking in quick bunches of words. In between the tumble of words I could hear her breathing hard. I could hear my father, too. His voice was low, almost growling. He sounded as if he had been drinking.

"Ty!" I called to Tyrone and heard him stir in his sleep. "Ty!"

"What?"

"They're arguing again," I said.

"What you waking me for?" Ty asked. I heard the rustle of the sheets as Ty slid back under the covers.

I looked at the digital numbers glowing on the dresser. It was 2:33 in the morning. I sat up, switched on the lamp near my bed, and looked around for my pants.

"Reuben, can you just tell me why?" Mom's voice was closer to the door. "The boys need their sleep!"

I got my pants up just as the door opened. For a moment I could see Reuben's shadow in the door frame. Then there was a click and the room was filled with light.

"Come on downstairs and help me to bring some stuff up," Reuben said. He was trying not to sound like he had been drinking, but I could see his eyes were red and I could smell his breath even from across the room.

I didn't say anything, just started pulling on my sneakers.

"You want something to eat?" Mom had changed her voice, made it softer.

Reuben shook his head and brushed past her as he left the room. She followed him.

It was 2:34. I heard the kitchen door open and shut and knew that Reuben had gone out.

I was still pulling on my shirt when I got out to the kitchen. There were two five-gallon cans of floor polish sitting by the kitchen table. Mom was sitting at the table, her head down. There was a cup on the table, and I could see it was half filled with coffee. She must have been up all night.

"You okay?" I asked.

"Yes," Mom said, turning her face away.

"He nervous?" I let the words float toward Mom, waited for an answer, and when none came I knew that Reuben had missed taking his pills again.

"Put on a jacket," Mom said. "It looks like rain."

"I'm okay. You going to wake up Ty?"

Mom nodded. "I'll wake him," she said. "If it's raining, come back and put on your jacket."

The summer heat was trapped in the stairwell, and the whole hall was heavy and smelly. I held my breath as I ran down the two flights to the street.

There were still a few people on the stoops. Somebody had a radio going, and a Spanish song bounced off the wall of the supermarket across the street. Down the block I saw Earl just closing up his used-furniture shop, pulling down the heavy steel gates.

I stood in the doorway for a long moment, watching Reuben unloading cans from a small, light-colored pickup truck. He was working quickly, the way he does when he's nervous, stiffly swinging the cans from the back of the truck onto the sidewalk. I knew the sweat would be dripping from his forehead and that there would be small drops of perspiration around his mouth.

"Start taking this stuff upstairs," he called to me. "Where's your brother?"

"Ty's coming," I answered.

He put down a can real hard and it made a clunking noise. Down the street a dog barked.

The cans were heavy. I took two, holding them by the

wire handles, and had to turn sideways as I went back into the hallway. Behind me I heard Reuben calling to me to get Ty downstairs to help. I mumbled that I would under my breath.

I stopped on the second floor to rest for a few seconds and shake my hands because they were getting numb. I heard somebody coming down the stairs. Tyrone.

"What's up?" Ty asked.

"He brought some stuff home in a truck," I answered.

"Where he get it from?"

"How do I know?"

Ty was older than me, but not that much taller. He jerked his shoulders as he went past me down the stairs.

It took four trips by me and four by Ty to get all of the cans into the apartment. After the last one, Ty and me stood on the sidewalk as Reuben tried to start the truck. It was getting cold. A light breeze picked up papers from the street and danced them down the block. A bus hissed its way across town toward Frederick Douglass Boulevard.

We were still on the stoop when the truck finally started and jerked away from the curb.

"How come Mom's crying?" Ty asked. "He hit her again?"

"I don't think so," I said. "He brought the stuff home in Mr. Kerlin's truck. Maybe it was about that."

"He's just jive," Ty said.

"I don't know."

"Yeah, you know."

In the apartment Mom looked up from the table to see who was coming in. She asked if Reuben was coming.

"He went off with the truck," Ty said. "If he's got any more stuff to bring up, you can tell him to bring it up by himself."

Mom started to say something, then stopped and picked up the cold coffee.

"Are you okay?" I asked her again when Ty went back to the bedroom.

"I'm okay, baby," she said.

I had thought the crying was over when Reuben first came home from the hospital. He had been away for nearly three months, and Mom had cried herself to sleep each night. It was the second time he had been in the hospital.

When he came home, I had asked Ty what was wrong with him.

"He's just messed up," Ty had answered. "Like a whole bunch of other guys walking round the hood talking to themselves. No big deal."

"He's our father," I said.

"No, man, he's Reuben," Ty said. "You forgot that?"

There had been a time when we called him Daddy. But when he started to act strange, he told me and Ty to call him by his name, Reuben. He said that we weren't his children, that he didn't have any children. Ty got mad but Mom and me cried. She was sad, and

I was sad and scared.

The first time I knew Reuben had a problem was once when we came home and he was scrubbing down the walls. He had cleaned a square as big as the door and then carefully drawn a line around it with a Magic Marker. Mom asked him what he was doing, and he had said that he was "taking care of business." He spent the rest of the day scrubbing the walls and marking off where he had cleaned. That was the first time I saw the sweating, too. He looked like a crack head but I didn't think he used crack.

Mom said not to worry about it, that he was just nervous, but I worried about it a lot. At first I tried to just ignore it, like it was no big thing, but then one day he started throwing dishes out the window, saying that they had a layer of poison on them. The neighbors called the police, and they arrested him. Then he was taken to the hospital.

At the hospital they had given him pills so he wouldn't be so nervous, but he didn't like to take them. We knew when he wasn't taking them, because he would start working real hard around the house. The working would become frenzied, and he would get more and more upset. Sometimes he would argue with Mom. Sometimes he threatened to hit her. Just thinking he might hit her was as bad as his doing it, or at least it was for me.

Most of the time he didn't have a regular job, just day work here and there, but he always had some kind of job to do. Mom thought he might get better if he had a steady job, but she hadn't expected Mr. Kerlin to hire him. Mom had been working with the Matthew Henson Community Project to build a neighborhood homeless shelter. It was supposed to be a place that people in the neighborhood would run, feeding the hungry and making a temporary shelter for the homeless. The only person in the neighborhood against the shelter was Mr. Kerlin. He owned the building the committee wanted to buy. Then he hired Reuben, which was weird and hard to think about.

"He's as clever as a snake in a silk suit," Mom said.

I liked that.

Sometimes I was afraid of Reuben, afraid that when he looked at me, he was seeing somebody he didn't like.

Morning. Mom came to the door and turned on the light. She called Ty's name softly, and he woke up.

"There's somebody on the phone for you," Mom said. "He won't give his name."

Ty got up and started to the phone in his underwear. Mom took a piece of lint from Ty's hair as he passed her.

"You sleep okay?" Mom asked me.

"I don't know," I answered. "I was asleep."

"You know, I was as young and stupid as you were once," she said, smiling. "You in the mood for buttermilk pancakes this morning?"

"Do I have to go to the store and get the stuff to make it?"

"You know, David, when I was your age, I used to love to go to the store for my mother."

"That's because you were a girl," I said.

"You get regular pancakes," Mom said as she left the room.

Tyrone came back to the room. He started getting dressed.

"What's up?" I asked him.

"That was Neil," he said. "He said a guy down the street has the first Spider-Man comic."

"How do you know it's the first one?"

"It's listed in the books," Ty said, lacing up his sneaks. "On the bottom it says 'The Chameleon Strikes!' and it has 1 March on it."

"How much is it worth?"

"Depends on the condition. If it's halfway decent it could be over a thousand dollars, but the guy in the store might not know that. That's why I'm going over there."

Collecting comic books was the only thing that Ty did that was like a kid. He was seventeen but he acted like he was twenty or more. He looked more like Reuben than I did, and sometimes when he got mad, he looked even more like our father. He thought he looked like Malcolm X, and he did a little, but only when he wore sunglasses.

When I was a kid he used to teach me things, and

sometimes he would even let me go bowling with him and his friends. When Reuben started changing, I was so busy thinking about what was going on, I didn't think much about Ty. Then, when I started looking at him, it was like he always had something else on his mind. Even when he talked to me, I thought he might be thinking about something else.

I didn't want to ask Ty about Reuben. Reuben had said that Ty was "testing" him, was checking him out. Sometimes it seemed that way. And even though I didn't want to ask Ty what he thought was going to happen with Reuben, I did.

"He's going to get into somebody's face that don't care if he's crazy," Ty said, "and they're going to bust a cap in his head."

"Nobody's going to shoot him," I said.

"He go around people acting crazy and sooner or later either somebody from the street or the Man is going to blow him away," Ty said. "And they won't care if he's crazy or not."

Mom came back in the room and asked him if he wanted some pancakes. He said no, that he had to go somewhere.

"Where you going so early?" Mom asked Ty.

"Round the way," he answered. He was checking out his hair in the small mirror on the cabinet door.

"And just where is 'round the way'?" Mom asked.

Ty didn't say anything, just gave Mom a look.

"Boy, you don't live in my house, eat my food, and don't answer me when I talk to you!" Mom had one hand on her hip and was shaking the other one at Ty.

"I'm going downtown," Ty said. "I don't need an investigation on the thing."

We heard a key in the door and everybody got quiet in a hurry. We all went into the kitchen, where Mom had been making coffee. She cut off the flame, then put the pot on a back burner and turned it on just as Reuben came through the door.

"You must have smelled the coffee," Mom said. "You hungry?"

"I was out working all night," Reuben said, taking off his jacket. "Naturally I'm hungry. Where you going, Tyrone?"

"Downtown," Ty said.

"Where downtown?" Reuben put his leg over the back of the chair and sat down.

"Just downtown," Ty said.

"I'm going to ask you one more time," Reuben said. "Where you going?"

"I got to see somebody about a job," Ty said.

Reuben looked at Ty hard, but Ty didn't look back.

I listened to see if he was going to slam the door. He didn't.

"What you doing today, David?"

"Me?"

"Anybody else in here named David?"

"I don't know," I said. "Maybe hang out with Loren. Or with Sessi and Kimi."

"David said that Sessi is building an African house on the roof," Mom said as she poured coffee into a cup in front of Reuben.

"They're living in the United States, they should be building an American house." Reuben hunched his shoulders forward like he does sometimes. "You want to go to the Bronx with me this afternoon? I'm going to take a nap and then go up to the Bronx and get some locks."

"Okay."

Reuben had put sugar in his coffee and stirred just the top of it. Sometimes Mom told him to stir the bottom so the sugar would go through the coffee but this time she didn't. The little lines in her forehead were there when she sat down.

"Did Mr. Kerlin ask you to bring David?"

Reuben looked at Mom from the side of his eyes and shook his head. "Why is Mr. Kerlin going to ask me to bring David?" he asked.

"I don't know," Mom said. "I just asked."

"If the boy doesn't want to come with me, he doesn't have to come," Reuben said. "Tyrone is the one who should be coming. How old is he? Seventeen? When I was seventeen I was in the army. Fort Dix, New Jersey. He needs a job. The boy's got too much time on his hands. I guess you think he's too good to be working for Mr. Kerlin."

"I don't think that anybody is too good to work for Mr. Kerlin," Mom said. "I know it's just a coincidence that you are working for Mr. Kerlin. I just wish he hadn't decided to renovate that building after all this time."

"What do you think you got a building for?" Reuben asked. "You think he's supposed to let it sit up there empty?"

"Reuben, I don't want to go into this again," Mom said. I could hardly hear her. "I'm just disappointed, that's all."

"Disappointed in him or in me?"

"Reuben, please."

Reuben got up, and I could see Mom get tense and hold her breath. "David, you go hang with your friends," Reuben said. "I'll go to the Bronx by myself."

Reuben left the kitchen, and he did slam the door to his and Mom's bedroom. I looked over at Mom and she was close to crying. I put my hand on hers and she got out a little smile. It wasn't much of a smile, but it was better than nothing.

"I'm going to be working at the beauty parlor today," Mom said. "Do you and Loren have any plans?"

"Maybe we'll just go downtown and take care of some business," I said.

"You and Loren better not have any business you have to take care of downtown," Mom said. "And you better find your way home as soon as Loren has to go home. I'll call to check on you, too."

I went downstairs with Mom and walked her to the

subway. When I asked her if she was mad at Reuben, she just shook her head and put her finger on my lips. I knew she didn't want to talk about it, but even if you didn't talk about it you couldn't help thinking about it.

I waited until Mom's train came and then went to Loren's house. Loren's mother does yoga, which is cool. She can do things like stand on her head and put her legs behind her head. Loren can stand on his head, too. That's the only thing he can do better than me.

Mrs. Hart, Loren's mother, gave me some yogurt to eat. She usually has two kinds of yogurt. Some with fruit in it, that is pretty good, and some with nothing in it, which I don't like. The kind she had was with fruit, and Loren and I both had a cup. Then she asked us to take a book downtown to the Countee Cullen Library on 136th Street.

"So what do you want to do today?" Loren asked when we were on the street.

"Since we're going downtown, we can go to the YMCA and play some pool," I said. "You got your Y card?"

"Yeah, but I got to be home early because my cousin is coming up from Philadelphia," Loren said. "He's grown, but my mother wants me to be there and act like we're family and everything."

"If he's your cousin, you are family."

"I know, but I don't have to act like it if I don't really know the dude," Loren said. "He used to play baseball in the minor leagues. You want to come and meet him?"

"I think I have to be home early, too," I said. "My dad asked me if I wanted to go to the Bronx with him. Then he said I didn't have to go, but you know how he is."

"That's funny, man," Loren said. "Because your mother is trying to get that building for the homeless people, and my mom says that your father is, like, her enemy."

"He's not the enemy," I said. "He's okay if he takes his pills."

We took the book back to the library, checked out what new videos they had, and then went to the playground. When we got to the basketball court, Randy and Clyde Johnson were there and we challenged them to a two-on-two game. Randy didn't want to play but Clyde did. Randy didn't want to play because he knew they were going to lose. And he was right. Me and Loren beat Randy and Clyde three games in a row.

There were spots of blood in the sink this morning. I ran the water and washed them away. It scared me, seeing that blood, and for a moment I could hardly think. Then, for some reason, I began to think of just crazy words. *Bink. Dink. Fink. Gink. Link. Mink. Pink. Rink.*

I leaned against the wall until I calmed down, then went back to my room and got dressed as fast as I could.

Reuben was asleep when I was leaving. He made noises as he slept, deep-breathing noises that weren't a snore but sounded more like a person who was working hard at just breathing. I didn't call Loren. I just went to his house and asked him if he wanted to go to the park. He said yes. He didn't say anything but he knew I was upset. I wished he was my brother. Ty was all right, but he was growing away from me. Mom said that people grow away from each other. She said it like it was something natural, and I wanted to tell her that I thought I was growing toward her, but I didn't.

We went over to the playground, checked out a ball, and shot around. We didn't play one-on-one because I didn't feel like getting hacked to death, which is what Loren does when he plays ball. We played two games of H-O-R-S-E and I won the first, but he won the second by pure luck. Loren was my best friend, but he couldn't play ball. The only reason he won at all was because of this strange-looking dude who came and sat down on the park bench to watch us.

"I think that guy is a scout for the NBA," Loren said. "Only he's in disguise."

"If he's a scout, they must have a homeless team," I said.

The man was dark, darker than Sessi. But while Sessi had dark hair, the man who watched us had white hair and a stubbly beard. He was dressed in a dirty brown overcoat, even though it was the middle of July and hot as anything. His pants, what I could see of them, were baggy and wrinkled. His shoes were black, but they didn't look too bad.

"I'm going to say something to him," Loren said.

"You better leave him alone," I said. "In case he's a mass murderer or something."

"He couldn't catch me," Loren said.

"Okay, suppose he used to be a track star and then became a mass murderer."

"He still couldn't catch me," Loren said. "Anyway, he probably just comes to the park to sleep."

Me and Loren sat on the bench, and the man, who had walked around the edge of the court, sat at the other end. He looked over at us and nodded, and Loren nodded back.

"Ty said he knows a guy who has the first issue of Spider-Man comics," I said. "He said it's worth a thousand dollars. You think anybody would ever pay that much for a comic?"

"I would if Ty said it was worth a thousand dollars."

"Suppose he's wrong?"

"I'll probably be a millionaire," Loren said. "A thousand dollars is just chump change to a millionaire."

"Ty's wrong about a lot of things. He thinks my father's crazy."

Loren didn't say anything, which was the wrong answer. I wondered what he thought, and what his parents were saying about Reuben. The sky was bright over the bridge in the distance, and gray over where me and Loren sat in the park.

"Here comes the scout," Loren said. "Watch me go right from the sixth grade to the NBA."

The old man had gotten up and was headed for us. He looked us up and down like we were looking him up and down.

"You guess how old I am, I'm going to give you five cents apiece," he said.

I thought maybe I had seen him before, and maybe not. He didn't have the kind of face you would remember, more of an old person's face, with lines and gray hairs and eyes that squinched out at you. He looked liked he had always been old.

"You boys guess how old I am, and I'll give you five cents each," he repeated.

"You're about fifty," Loren said.

I would have guessed even older than that, because he looked like the pictures of the Ancient Mariner we had in our English book, only he was black. His eyes were funny too, as if he wasn't looking at what was in front of him but at something far away. His beard was part white and part gray, and I had never seen the little cap he wore on anybody else.

"What you say?" He pointed a finger at me.

"I'll say fifty-eight," I said, more to be saying something than believing it.

"Old Moses is three hundred and three years old!" he said. "Can you believe that?"

"No," Loren said.

"Well, I am," the man said. He nodded to himself like he was thinking about being so old. "What names you boys got?"

"My name is Mr. Hart," Loren said. "I'm a combination rap star and pro ballplayer. This guy here is Mr.

Curry. He's my agent."

"Pleased to meet you, Mr. Hart, and pleased to meet you, Mr. Curry." He bowed forward from the waist. "My name is Moses Littlejohn. You can call me Moses."

"You want to play some one-on-one?" Loren asked.

"Leave him alone," I said. "He's probably crazy or something."

"Crazy? What is crazy?" the old man asked. "What would crazy be for a black man?"

He looked up at the sky and kind of pulled at his chin.

"It means that you're not wrapped too tight," Loren said.

"I knew a man once who they called crazy," the old man said. "He wasn't crazy—he was just piling up his being mad. He'd get mad about this and he'd put it on the pile. Then he'd get mad about that and he'd pile that on the pile. And then he'd get mad at something else. You see how that goes. And after a while all that mad got to falling in on itself and collapsing until the point where you couldn't tell what he was mad at and neither could he. Since it was too much trouble straightening it all out, people just decided to call him crazy. Here, let me see that basketball."

Loren tossed the ball to the man and watched as he took it and bounced it a couple of times. You could see right away he had never been a ballplayer, because he couldn't dribble. Then he kind of half walked, half shuffled out onto the court and threw the ball up toward the basket. I watched it as it hit the rim and bounced onto the court.

The old man laughed like that was the funniest thing in the world.

"You drink too much wine to make a basket," Loren said.

"Wine?" The old man was suddenly serious. "You looking, boy, but you ain't seeing. No, you ain't seeing nothing at all."

When Loren looked over at me he was still grinning, but I don't like to laugh at old people. The man came back to the bench and sat down while Loren picked up the ball and shot it. He made two baskets in a row and looked over to see if I had seen him.

"Loren's okay," I said.

"You young people are all okay," the man said as Loren came over and sat down next to me.

"So what do you do?" I asked.

"He don't play basketball," Loren said.

"Well, that's true," the old man said. "What I do is to carry these dreams of mine. You ever carry a dream?"

"How old did you say you were?" I asked him.

"Three hundred, maybe three hundred and nine," he said. "I hope you don't believe that. You don't, do you?"

"No," I said.

"Well, you know I'm thankful for that. I thought you two looked too sensible to believe it," he said. "You got to be careful what you believe these days."

"If you were three hundred years old, you would have been dead a long time ago," Loren said.

"If I was your ordinary man, I would have been dead," Mr. Moses said. "But I was given the gift of bearing dreams when I was about—how old are you, young fellow?"

"Twelve," Loren answered.

"Well, I can't remember exactly when, but it must have been about your age," Mr. Moses said. "I was sitting on the side of the road one day, when a fellow come up to me the same way I come up to you. He told me his name and claimed he was four hundred years old. I squinted up one eye and looked him over real carefully."

Mr. Moses cocked his head to one side and was squinting one eye. "Then what happened?" I asked.

"He told me he was a dream bearer, that he had been carrying dreams for hundreds of years." The old man stopped looking at me and Loren, and his vision seemed to drift away. The change in his face surprised me, because he had turned from just interesting to unbelievably sad. "He told me he was tired and needed to pass his dreams on to somebody new. Then he asked me if I wanted to take them."

"And you said yeah," Loren said.

"Now, how was I going to say that when I didn't a bit more believe him than you believe me?" Mr. Moses said.

"Then how come you call yourself a dream bearer?" Loren asked.

"'Cause the more I listened to Aaron—that was his name—the more sense he made. It wasn't just the words that made sense—it got to where I could feel what he was talking about. Feel it deep in my bones."

"So how you get to be three hundred and three years old?" I asked.

"Did I say three hundred and three? It could be three hundred and eleven, maybe three hundred and twelve. I know I'm old."

"I still don't believe it," Loren said.

"Phew-oo!" He took out a bright yellow handkerchief and wiped his brow. "I'm sure glad I'm not dealing with stupid people."

"If you don't want us to believe it, why are you telling us?" I asked.

Mr. Moses looked at me, wiped his brow again, then folded his handkerchief carefully and put it into his pocket. "You know, even a strong man gets tired," he said. "And I am one tired man. I've been looking almost two years for someone to give my gift to, somebody young and strong. Like you young men."

"I don't dream," Loren said. "I just go to bed, go to sleep, and then wake up in the morning."

"You know what a dream is?" the old man asked.

"Sure," Loren said. "It's like you're sleeping and you think something is going on, but it's not, it's only a dream."

"And how do you know you're not dreaming this life you're leading?"

"If Loren was dreaming, he'd win against me one-on-one," I said.

"You got your dreams in your pockets?" Loren asked.

"In here!" Mr. Moses tapped the side of his head. "If I had them in my pocket, I could take them out and put them down for a while. Then I wouldn't be so tired. You carry dreams in your head and it just makes you tired. Just makes you tired."

"And that makes you want to rest all the time?" Loren said. "Right?"

"No, it makes me want to journey on, son, trying to leave the dreams behind me."

"I have to go," I said.

"Well, look at how the time is passing," Mr. Moses said. "So long, Mr. Hart and Mr. Curry."

"You can call me David."

"David? Ain't that a good name! Good-bye, Mr. David. And you can call me Moses." He touched his hat like he was going to take it off, but he didn't.

"I think he's strange," Loren said as we left the playground. "My father said that when he was young, they used to have strange people in the circus and charge a quarter to go see them. Now they just turn them loose so they can bother everybody. And I know he's not three hundred years old, either. What do you think?"

"I don't know," I said. "Sometimes old people say funny things."

On the way home I didn't think about the old man but about what Loren had said about strange people not being locked up. I knew Loren wasn't talking about my father, but he could have been. My father wasn't crazy, Mama had said, but he was troubled.

I also thought about what the old man had said about going on with his journey to leave his dreams behind.

The loud banging on the front door woke me up. The first thing I thought was that it was Reuben, either drunk or nervous, not finding his keys. Then I heard his voice and he was asking who it was at the door. Even through our bedroom door I heard a man's voice say it was the police.

I turned on the light and looked over at Tyrone's bed. He was sleeping with the covers pulled up over his head. The banging got louder. I looked at the clock on the dresser. One thirty. I heard Mama talking, but I couldn't hear what she was saying.

"Ty!" I got up and shook his leg.

Ty raised himself on one elbow without opening his eyes.

The banging on the door got louder, and Ty opened his eyes.

"What's going on?" he asked.

"The police are banging on the door," I said.

The banging got louder, and the police were yelling for somebody to open the door before they tore it down. Reuben was yelling back, saying he didn't want anybody in his house. I felt sick to my stomach.

Ty was awake and listening to the all the noise. Then he jumped out of bed, took something from under the mattress, and left the room. A moment later I heard the toilet flush once, and then again. Tyrone got back to our room just as I heard the police come in.

"Get in bed!" he said.

I put my pants on and opened the door. From where I stood, I could see three guys, two white and one black. They had their guns out and a flashlight was shining in my face.

"Keep your hands where I can see them!" the black guy said to me.

The cops told Mama to get everybody out into the kitchen, and she went and got Ty. The cops made us stand around the kitchen table with our hands in front of our chests with the palms toward them. Mama had her robe on, but Reuben was in his shorts and a T-shirt. The cops asked Mama if they could search the house.

"It'll make things easier for you." The tallest of the three cops was a light-brown-skinned guy wearing a sweatshirt. His badge was on a chain around his neck.

"No, you can't search my house!" Reuben was just about shouting. "You don't have any business in here."

"Are you 'Circle T'?" one of the white cops asked Ty.

"And don't lie to me or I'll make you wish you hadn't."

Whack! Whack!

Reuben was slamming his fist into the palm of his hand.

"You'd better relax, buddy!" the black cop said.

Whack! Whack!

Reuben looked really mad as he punched his hand again.

"He's on medication," Mama said.

Reuben turned toward the stove and started turning the burners on.

"Are you dealing—" The cop started to talk to Ty but then turned to back to Reuben. "What did you do that for?"

Reuben's eyes were puffed out and his mouth was tight. Mama put her hand on his arm, and he smacked it away hard.

"We can cuff you if we have to—" one of the cops said.

Reuben started cursing and saying they better have their guns out if they were going to mess with him.

The policemen looked like they didn't know what to do, and then the shortest one said they should come back with a warrant and arrest the whole family.

"You'd better stay out of the Thirty-fifth Precinct." One of the cops pointed his finger at Ty. "If I'm the one who catches you dealing, I'm going to find a reason to blow you away."

The cops backed out of the apartment, and Mama went to the stove and turned off the burners.

"Why you tell them I was on medication?" Reuben asked.

"I just didn't want anybody hurt," Mama said.

"I can't be a man in my own house." Reuben had turned and was talking to me and Ty. "She got to give me an excuse! I got to be on medication!"

"Boys, go to bed." Mama's voice was tired.

"Why they got to go to bed?" Reuben asked.

"Reuben, it's late." Mama sat down at the end of the table.

"Anybody can walk in my house and tell my family what to do." Reuben's voice was getting higher and he was holding his chin up like he was having trouble breathing. "Just walk right in like they own the place because there ain't no man in here to stop them."

"I have to go to work in the morning. . . ." Mama stood up and was shaking her head.

Tyrone left the kitchen first. There was a plate on the drainboard and Mama picked it up, rinsed it off, and put it in the dish rack. Reuben turned and started talking to the wall. I heard him saying he might as well talk to the wall because nobody was listening to him anyway.

Mama looked at him for a while, then shook her head and started for the bedroom. Then I heard her talking to Ty. She was telling him not to go out, that it was danger-ous. Ty said he had to go somewhere, and a moment later he came into the kitchen and was opening the door.

"Where you going?" By the time Reuben got the words out, Ty was already out the door.

Mama stood in the doorway between the kitchen and the parlor. There were tears running down her face, and she didn't even try to stop them. When she looked at me, I wanted to cry, too. It was like she wanted me to say something and I didn't know what to say. She turned and went into the bedroom. Reuben sat down at the kitchen table and was muttering to himself. I felt so tired, I didn't think my legs would move.

I never felt so bad in my life. It was as if sadness had just come in and was living with our family. When things were going wrong, it didn't seem so bad with all the doors closed and it was all stuff that you could keep indoors. But when the police came, everybody in the building knew it. When they came in the door, it was like they were opening you up for the world to see. I didn't know if Ty had done anything, but just thinking he might have made me mad.

I pulled the cover over my head and just tried to shut out everything.

Morning came and Ty wasn't home. Mama was making eggs. Reuben was hunched over a cup of coffee. He was dressed, but his hair wasn't combed.

"The light in the living room is out," Mama said. "It's probably the bulb."

"People don't have a right to come into your apartment without a search warrant," Reuben said without looking up from his coffee. "That's the cops or nobody else."

"Reuben, I'm sorry about last night," Mama said.

"You didn't do anything wrong," I said.

"Everything's up in the air because I got a job," Reuben said. "That's what's going on. Everybody's nervous because a black man has a job."

"It hasn't got anything to do with your job or you," Mama said. "Somebody must have told them that Tyrone was involved with drugs."

"That's them," Reuben said. "But they didn't come in here excusing themselves for being cops or for saying something about Tyrone. They just bust in here like they owned the world. And what you do? What you do?"

"What *did* I do?" Mama asked.

"You start making excuses for me," Reuben said. "You can go after whatever you want with this homeless place but I can't even take a job."

"Reuben, I don't need this conversation this morning," Mama said. "Do you know that your son didn't come home last night?"

"Yeah, I know it," Reuben said. "I'll talk to him today."

"Do you want eggs this morning?"

"You been making excuses for me ever since I started working for Mr. Kerlin," Reuben went on. "Like I'm some kind of freak or something."

"Reuben, I am too tired, and too beat down, to carry this burden this morning," Mama said. "Can we just rest it for today?"

"What you know about Mr. Kerlin anyway? You ever talk to him? You ever sit down and have a face-to-face conversation with the man?" Reuben asked. "You say all he's interested in is the money. What's he supposed to be interested in? He's a businessman and he got an apartment building to rent out. What's he supposed to do?"

"Do you want eggs?"

"No, I don't want no eggs," Reuben said.

"You know as well as I do that the building at Three sixty-nine sat there empty and run-down for nine years, Reuben," Mama said. "David, do you want these eggs?"

Mama cracked two eggs and put them in a bowl, sprinkled them with basil and salt, and stirred them with a fork.

"The junkies and the crack heads were living in there last year and stealing the pipes," Mama said. "You said that yourself."

"That was last year!" Reuben said.

"That was last year, before the community decided to buy the building from the city to make a shelter," Mama said. "Now he's fighting us and saying the city doesn't own the building because he's paying off his taxes. Everybody knows he's not interested in that building. He's just trying to keep us from doing something with it."

"The neighborhood is coming up," Reuben said. "You

even got rich people moving in over at the Riverfront Houses."

"I haven't seen any rich people moving into Riverfront, and even if it is true, they're not going to be moving into Three sixty-nine, which is Mr. Kerlin's house. David, didn't I ask you if you wanted these eggs?"

"Yes, ma'am."

The eggs were scrambled and Mama put them on my plate.

"Mr. Kerlin's got a dream," Reuben said.

"Lord, if I hear that 'I got a dream' phrase one more time, I'm going to scream," Mama said. "I wish Martin Luther King had never made that speech."

Reuben stood up real quick, and his chair fell backward onto the kitchen floor.

"Reuben!" Mama backed away.

"What?"

"You—you want some toast?"

Reuben didn't answer. He just looked down at the table and then, with one big swing, he knocked the coffeepot, the salt and pepper shakers, and his cup off the table. His coffee ran over the plastic tablecloth toward me and I stopped it with the tea towel. He grabbed his jacket off the chair and went out the door, slamming it hard behind him.

Mama started picking up things from the floor and I started to help.

"Be careful," she said. "Don't cut yourself."

"You okay?" I asked.

"As okay as I get these days," she said.

When Mom got mad, she got quiet. When Reuben got mad, he would do something physical, like slam a door or knock something off a table. No matter how upset Mom was, it never stayed with her, she could always get up a smile after a while. With Reuben it seemed to always stay, and I thought about him piling it up higher and higher.

Last night he hit Ty. Ty came in late, after nine, and Mama started in about where he had been. Ty went to the refrigerator and opened it, and Mama asked him again where he had been.

"Taking care of business," Ty said.

That's when Reuben stood up and hit Ty. He didn't just hit him, he knocked him away from the refrigerator and onto the floor. Mama screamed. Reuben sat down, put his elbows on the table, and leaned forward against his clasped hands. He looked right at Ty sitting stunned on the linoleum floor. Ty was unsteady as he got up and said something about "getting out of this stupid house." I could see he was hurt. His hands were shaking and he was holding on to the cabinet. Mama ran and grabbed him and hugged him real close. Then she took him into our bedroom.

When I went into the bedroom, Ty was asleep. I lay across the bed thinking about what had happened, about the hurt expression on Ty's face as he sat on the kitchen floor after Reuben hit him. I had almost fallen asleep when I heard Reuben's footsteps in the hall. I held my breath as I heard the door open. Reuben looked over to where Ty lay. He watched him for a while, then turned toward me.

"You want to give me a hand at the job tomorrow?" His voice was low, easy.

"Okay," I said.

No, I said to myself. I didn't feel any better about it in the morning, either. But there was no way I was going to say no to Reuben.

Some of the buildings on 145th Street are nice, especially as you go toward the hill. The block between Malcolm X and Frederick Douglass is beat-up and kind of run-down. Down the street, across from the church, there are some buildings that have been fixed up. The workers, mostly West Indian dudes with Rasta dreads and thick accents, worked on them for over six months. Loren has a friend who moved into one of the buildings after it was fixed up, and we went to his house and saw how they had painted everything and patched up all the cracks. They had put in brand-new bathrooms and new kitchens, and Loren's friend, whose name was Ollie, was real proud of it. Mr. Kerlin's house at three sixty-nine was different.

"All you need in a house is the basic structure," Reuben said. We had finished taking the garbage from the fourth floor and putting it into big, black plastic garbage bags. "You get the basic structure and then you can fix up each apartment like you want it. Jimmy Carter—you know who Jimmy Carter is?"

"He used to be president."

"Right. He's fixing up places for people all over the country. He just fixes up the outside so the rain don't come in," Reuben said. "Then it's up to the people to fix the insides themselves. You know what I mean?"

"Yes."

"That's what Mr. Kerlin's doing. Your mama don't understand that. She thinks he needs to fix up the whole insides. But if you do that, then you got to charge big money for the rent. You see any old photographs or anything like that, you need to put them aside. We can sell them to Earl or Akbar down the street."

We collected the garbage, mostly stuff people had left behind when they moved, and put it in the bags. I was working as fast as I could, but I wasn't working as fast as Reuben. He was working hard and fast, and the sweat was pouring off him. I thought of what Mr. Moses had said about trying to leave your dreams behind.

"The building was empty a long time," I said.

"Harlem is full of empty buildings and empty promises," Reuben said. "Every time you see a building all boarded up, you're looking at a promise that somebody didn't keep."

"Oh." I didn't know what he meant, and I didn't want to ask. Sometimes when I talked to him, I didn't know what he was talking about and I didn't want him to get mad at me for asking.

"What you thinking about your brother?" he asked.

"He's probably in the streets too much," I said. "In school they said that if you hang in the streets too much, you start thinking like a street person."

"He dealing drugs?"

"Ty?" I looked at Reuben to see if he was serious, and he was. "I don't think he's dealing drugs."

Mr. Kerlin came by at six o'clock in the evening to see how things were going. He's light-brown-skinned and is always smoking a stinky cigar that he waves around when he's talking. When he agrees with what you're saying, he points that cigar at you. He doesn't say anything, just jabs that cigar in your direction. When he likes what he's said, he nods his head like he agrees with himself.

"You got a fine young man here," Mr. Kerlin said. "What's he going to be? An engineer? Maybe a lawyer?"

"David's going to be a pilot," Reuben said.

"Well, we can use some black pilots," Mr. Kerlin said. "Why did you decide to become a pilot, young man?"

"I thought it was a good job," I said. "And I like to travel."

"Using your head," Mr. Kerlin said. The cigar jabbed in my direction. "You keep using your head and you can do anything you want."

"I got the top two floors cleaned up," Reuben said. "If I work tomorrow, I can get the whole building cleaned by this coming Wednesday."

"Take your time," Mr. Kerlin said. "I need somebody in here so the junkies don't start ripping out the pipes again. You know they get up to eight cents a pound for copper."

"Yes, sir."

We worked most of the day. When we left, I was tired and so was Reuben. He stopped in a liquor store and I waited outside. When he came out, he had a dollar in his hand and he gave that to me. He said I had earned more than that one dollar but he would make it up to me later. He asked me if that was okay and I said that it was.

"If you see your brother dealing drugs, you got to let me know," Reuben said. "It's never wrong for us to look out for each other. You believe that?"

"I believe it," I said.

"And I don't want you messing around with no drugs," he went on. "You got a whole lot of sense in you, boy. Don't be leaving it in the streets."

When we got home, Mama had made spaghetti, and

Reuben had a little before he went to bed.

"How you doing, Mr. Bojangles?" Mama said when Reuben had left the room.

"Mr. Bojangles?"

"When I was a little girl, there was a song called 'Mr. Bojangles.' It was about this old man who used to dance and sing," Mama said. "I loved that song. When you were a baby, we used to call you Mr. Bojangles because you moved around so much."

"Mr. Kerlin came to the job today," I said. "He asked Reuben what I was going to be, and Reuben said I was going to be a pilot."

"What did you think about that?"

"I liked it," I said. "I had never thought of being a pilot, but that's something I would like to do."

"Is it phat?"

"Yeah, I guess it is."

We watched television for a while, a program about some kind of monkeys on some island, but I was too tired to make sense of it.

I had a lot to think about when I went to bed. I thought about Reuben asking me if Ty was messing with drugs. When the police had come to the house and Ty had flushed something down the toilet, I figured it was drugs but I didn't want to think about it. It was just out of my mind and I thought that nobody else knew anything about it, but Reuben must have been thinking about it.

Ty was into his own program and I knew it wasn't cool, and that sometimes Ty hung out with the wrong crowd. When Loren saw them hanging on the corner or selling drugs, he said that they were just forming their own freelance cell block.

"David, Mrs. Mutu called. They're having a problem," Mom said. "I'm going to go over there. Do you want to come with me?"

"Who called?"

"Mrs. Mutu—Sessi's mother."

On the way up to Sessi's house I asked Mom what kind of trouble they were having, and she said that they needed somebody to stand up for them as character references.

"They're getting married?" I asked.

"They're applying to become United States citizens," Mom said. "Since the terrorist attacks, the government has been scrutinizing everybody very carefully. Do you know what scrutinizing means?"

"Means looking them over carefully," I said. "Am I smart, or what?"

"Nice to know you have my genes," Mom said.

Sessi's apartment was the same as ours except the furniture was different and it was cleaner. Mr. Mutu opened the door and smiled and bowed as we came in. Then he asked us to come into the living room. There were family pictures on the wall and a picture of the church they had gone to in Kenya. A white lady sat in a chair near the window. She had a clipboard and a lot of papers on a small table near her. Sessi, Kimi, and Mrs. Mutu were sitting on the couch.

"This is Mrs. Goldklank, from the Immigration Service," Mrs. Mutu said. She smiled, but she didn't look that happy.

"The Mutu family has applied for citizenship and has completed most of the paperwork. For some reason they've neglected to provide the character references on this form, and they said that you might be willing to swear to their likelihood of becoming good citizens. They have two references and need one more. You won't be held responsible for them in any way, but we would like you to be as honest and straightforward as possible."

"I know the Mutu family from our local church, and they're lovely people," Mom said. "I'd be pleased to be a character witness."

"I'll be a witness for Sessi," I said.

"I think the Immigration Service is looking for adults,"

Mrs. Goldklank said. "But I will note that you volunteered. May I have your name?"

"David Curry."

"Mrs. Curry, have you always known the Mutu family to be self-supporting and, of course, not engaged in any criminal activity?"

"That's correct," Mom said. "I think they'll make outstanding Americans."

"If you'll write that on this form, I would appreciate it," Mrs. Goldklank said. She handed the paper to Mom, and Mom started reading it.

I looked over at Sessi and she looked really nervous. Her brother was nervous, too. Mr. Mutu was standing behind me, and I didn't want Mrs. Goldklank to see me turn and watch him.

After Mom finished reading the paper, she put it on her lap and asked for a pen.

"Thank you for asking me to be a character reference." This is what Mom said to Mrs. Mutu, which got Sessi's mother to crying right away.

When Mom had finished signing and given the papers back to the lady from Immigration, we had some tea, which I didn't like, and then me, Mom, and Mrs. Goldklank left together.

"Are they going to be granted citizenship?" Mom asked Mrs. Goldklank in the hallway.

"Mr. Mutu has a master's degree in journalism, so that stands in his favor. The problem is that the list of people applying for citizenship from Africa is *this* long." She held out her arms to show how long the list was. "Many of these people get discouraged from waiting so long and just drop out of sight. Eventually they're found and deported—and then they'll never get into this country legally."

"This country isn't that happy letting Africans in, is it?" Mom said.

Mrs. Goldklank stopped at the top of the stairs and looked at Mom for a long while. "We let people in who we are sure will become assets," she said. "We have enough problems of our own."

When Mom doesn't like something, she gets this look in her eyes. I knew that Mrs. Goldklank had said something that made her mad.

We got home and Reuben was reading the newspaper in the kitchen. Mom asked if he wanted anything to eat, and he didn't answer. Then she asked me if I wanted anything to eat and I said no, even though I was hungry. Mom said she had to get ready for work and went into the bathroom.

"Where you coming from?" Reuben asked.

"Just now?"

"Is it a secret?" He still didn't look up.

"No," I said. "Mrs. Mutu asked us to sign papers for her so she could become an American citizen. I don't know if they're going to let her be a citizen, but we signed the papers."

"Maybe somebody can sign some papers for me," Reuben said. "What kind of papers they got? Be an American? Be a New Yorker? Maybe they got some 'be respected' papers? You think they got those kind of papers?"

I shrugged. I didn't know what he was talking about.

Reuben sat looking at the newspaper—I don't think he was really reading it—until Mom left for work. Then he went into the bedroom and shut the door.

Reuben never hurt me, but he was away from me. Even when he was near, it was more like he was dealing with something else, a strange thing that was always with him. I didn't think I was like Reuben. Everything I had was just me, just what I was doing. I didn't think about funny stuff the way Reuben did, and I didn't have dreams like the old man.

Me and Ty got along all right until he started hanging out with the 147th Street posse. Most of the people on 145th Street were okay. It wasn't a great place to live, but we all got along. The main trouble was around the bicycle shop. The guys who ran the bicycle shop were from 147th Street, and some people said that they sold drugs.

The bicycle shop used to be a roti shop, where you could buy hot West Indian food. They also sold incense, sodas, and loose cigarettes. Then the man who owned the shop died and they boarded up the place. The people who started the bicycle shop didn't rent it or anything, they just broke the lock that kept it closed and started fixing bicycles in it. The police would come by and close them down, and it would stay closed for a week or so, then open up again and stay open for two or three months before the police came again.

Ty had another year of high school and was smart, but Mom said it didn't matter how smart he was if he got arrested or if he used drugs. She didn't say he was messing with drugs, but I think she thought he was. The night the police came to our house and asked if he was Circle T, she was really upset. When I asked her the next day if she thought that Ty was getting in trouble, she said no.

"He just needs to get away from this neighborhood for a while," she said. "When he goes to college, he'll see a different kind of life and see what's possible. That's all you and he need to see, what life really has to offer a young black man who is as smart as both of you are."

I knew that wasn't right, but it was what she had to say because she had just about as much bad stuff going on in her life as she could handle.

In school they had told us what to do when we thought someone we knew was getting involved in drugs. We were supposed to tell a teacher or our parents.

"And talk to the boy or girl you think might be using drugs," the principal had said at assembly. "Let them know that you don't approve of what they are doing. Sometimes just your letting them know what you think of what they are doing will be the turning point in their lives."

"If somebody is using crack," Loren had said, "I'm not telling on them. They're liable to go off and shoot me or something."

I didn't think Ty was going to shoot me, or hurt me. I wished I didn't have to think about it at all.

Loren is on punishment. His mom always says that if he believes something, he should stick up for it, but he has to have a logical argument. But when he gets into his argument, his mom gets mad and right away he's in trouble. Me and him were supposed to go up to the roof to see how Sessi's house was coming along, but he had to clean the bathroom. When Loren goes on punishment, it's always about cleaning the bathroom. He looked sad when I told him I was going to the playground to practice my free throws. He said when he finished he would come and find me.

"If it's all right with my mother," he added.

"Loren has to learn the difference between logical discussion and sarcasm," Mrs. Hart said.

Loren's mother is white and his father is black. There aren't many white people who live on 145th Street, but there are some who work at the supermarket across the street. Loren's father works in a bank, and I don't know where his mom works. She's got that look like she's ready for you to make a mistake, so maybe she's a teacher. Sometimes his parents run together in the park, which is cool. I knew that arguments didn't work with your parents, and that's what Loren had to learn.

It was hot when I reached the street. There was music blasting all over 145th Street. Usually when the music is that loud there's somebody out there dancing, but it was too hot even for the young girls to dance.

When I got to the basketball court, it was almost empty, too. At least no kids were playing on it. Gordito Lopez, who lived over on St. Nicholas Avenue, was there, and he was reading, as usual. Gordito was twelve and like a brainiac 2003. He was also too fat to play sports, which is why everybody called him Gordito. The only other person in the playground, over near the fence, was Mr. Moses. There was about one foot of shade in the park, and he was sitting in it. He looked like he was sleeping, but when I got near him he said hello.

"Nice to see a young man exercising his body," he said.

I made up a game in my head where I was playing for a college team. In the made-up game we were trailing by one point. I dribbled left, then right, then turned my back to the basket as the time wound down. I was on the foul line. Five seconds. Four seconds. Three . . . Two . . . I made a quick fake and then turned for the jumper! The ball was in the air as the buzzer sounded. It hit the back rim and bounced off. But I was fouled. Two shots. I missed the first one, then made the second. Overtime!

I went through the whole thing again. This time I missed both foul shots and sat down a little way from Mr. Moses.

"How is life treating you, David?" he asked.

"Okay," I said, surprised that he remembered my name. "How is life treating you, Mr. Moses?"

"Life is like a bowl of delicious black grapes," Mr. Moses said. "You ever have a big bowl of delicious, juicy grapes?"

"Sure."

"Then you know that life is truly wonderful," Mr. Moses said.

"What do you do all the time?" I asked.

"What does Moses Littlejohn do?" He scratched at his chin and looked up in the air as if he was trying to figure out what he did. "I eat a little, I work when I can find some that's easy on the back, but mostly I just carry my dreams from day to day."

"For all those years?" I sat a little way down from him on the park bench.

"That's right, for all those years."

"If you dream every night, that's got to be thousands of dreams to remember," I said. "You remember every dream you ever had?"

"No, I ain't got that many dreams," Mr. Moses said. "You see, regular dreams just come and go and you forget about them. But there are special dreams, dreams that fill up the soul, dreams that can be unfolded like wings and lift you off the ground. Those are the dreams I must bear."

"How many special dreams you got?" I asked.

"Five now," he said. "I used to have six, but one got away from me. That old man I told you about said that when I saw a dream getting away from me, it was time for me to move on and let somebody else do the carrying."

"How did a dream get away from you?"

"I was lying on my bed one day, full of my own thoughts and my own visions," he said. "I began thinking about one of my dreams, just mulling it over in my mind. Then, all of a sudden, I began not to understand what that dream was all about. I kept trying to put the pieces together again, but it didn't make sense anymore."

"What was the dream?" I asked.

"It was about people I thought I knew, friends who used to walk and talk with me, but then I didn't know them anymore, or what that dream was even doing in my head. Now ain't that something? Ain't that truly something?"

"So all you got is five dreams left?"

"All I got is five."

A pigeon landed in front of us and started pecking at a pizza crust someone had left on the ground. He pecked at it and followed it under the park bench as it moved away from him.

"Are all your dreams scary?" I asked.

"Sometimes they are. Sometimes a dream can be a dreadful thing—and sometimes . . ." A small smile came on his face and he clasped his hands together. "Sometimes it can be as soothing as water trickling down a Mississippi mountainside."

"Is that where you're from? Mississippi?"

"Ooo-whee! You are one quick young man. Yes, sir, that's where I'm from. Mound Bayou, Mississippi. You ever hear of Mound Bayou?"

"Nope."

The pigeon was still pushing the pizza crust around when a sparrow swooped down, grabbed the crust, and tried to fly away with it, but it fell from his beak back onto the ground.

"I bet you they got more pigeons in this city than they got people," Mr. Moses said.

"Why don't you tell me one of your dreams," I said.

Mr. Moses put his head back and closed his eyes. For a long while he didn't say anything. Then he started into what seemed a little like singing and a little like moaning. It sounded sad, but it sounded enough like music to make me think that he was going to put some words to it. Then he stopped singing, hunched forward, and put his hands on his knees.

"I got me a dream that's as old as me and older," he said. "In the dream I ain't nothin' but a child. Maybe five, or maybe six, or maybe even seven. I'm watching some people chain down my father and I hear him howling. Lord, I hear him howling!"

Mr. Moses' body shook all over, and he shook his head back and forth. I looked down at where Gordito was sitting and saw him looking at me and Mr. Moses.

"When they done chained him down, they picked him up, chains and all, and carried him down by the water-side," Mr. Moses spoke in a low voice, almost whispering. "The tide was in and the whitecaps were foaming and flickering in the sun. The water washed up on the beach and slid back into the sea. Up and back. Up and back, like it was reaching for something on the shore. I was watching my daddy howling and I howled with him.

"Somebody was saying we was all going into the ocean. Another poor person was crying out for mercy. I was too scared to cry out—I was just looking as they took my father on the boat. In the dream I can see his mouth gaped open like a dead man's mouth and I can hear him howling and the sound of the water rushing against the shore. Oh Lord, ain't that something. Ain't that a dream for you?"

Mr. Moses shook his head and looked away from me. He didn't say anything after that and I didn't say anything either. I was thinking about his dream and trying not to think about it at the same time. Then Loren came. When I saw Loren, I told Mr. Moses I had to leave.

"Good to see you this morning," he said. "You sure

look like a sensible young man this morning."

He smiled, and I saw he had some teeth missing on one side but the teeth he had were nice and white.

"Are you a homeless guy?" I asked.

"There ain't no homeless people, David," he said. "There's just people ain't in their homes."

"Oh. Okay."

I met Loren at the far end of the court, and he asked me if I wanted to play some ball and I said no, it was too hot, and we decided to walk over to Riverside Drive.

"How come you were on punishment?" I asked.

"It was about you," Loren said. "I told my mother that you and your mom went over Sessi's house to be character references, and she said that Sessi's mom had called her, too, but she didn't go."

"Why?"

"She said she wasn't sure if they should let everybody into the country just because they want to come over here," Loren said. "I said she just didn't like Africans. That's what I said."

"What did she say?"

"Clean the bathroom."

"She let you come out, so that's okay," I said.

"You were talking to the old man?"

"Yeah."

"What did he say?"

"He told me about a dream," I said.

"I think you take him too serious," Loren said.

"Yeah, maybe."

Me and Loren walked along the park, and he was talking about the two of us going to the movies later in the week. We both liked the movies and picked four that we wanted to see.

The whole time I was talking to Loren, I was thinking about Mr. Moses and the dream that got away from him. I had never lost a dream like that. I had never really had a dream that was so much a part of me as the old man's dreams. But I was thinking that there were things that were getting away from me, and people I thought I knew who now weren't so clear. Mr. Moses never asked me anything about myself, but I wondered what he knew.

"He can live in the streets for all I care," Reuben said.

"Well, I don't want him living in the streets," Mom said. "Whatever he's doing, he's my son. And he's going to be my son for as long as I am alive."

They were talking about Ty. He hadn't been home for two days. The police hadn't come to the house, so I thought he was okay, but I wasn't sure. Reuben was acting like he didn't care.

I knew my brother, at least I had thought I knew him before he started acting so strange. Now every night I would wake up, turn on the light, and look at his empty bed. I wanted to hear him grunt and pull the cover over his head, the way he did sometimes, or ask me if I was crazy waking him up in the middle of the night. I wanted him to be the old Ty, acting like he was tired of me hanging around him all the time. The thought of Ty living on the street gave me a nervous feeling inside. But it was almost as if I was the one who wasn't home, instead of him.

Mr. Moses had said that there were no homeless people, just people who weren't in their homes. I liked that, but I didn't know if it made a real difference. I thought Mr. Moses was not in his home, and now Ty wasn't in his.

I heard Mom talking on the phone to Ira. Ira played saxophone when he could find work, and sometimes he taught or drove a cab. Mom told Ira that Ty was running the streets and asked him to give her a call if he saw him.

When Mom was happy, her voice sounded full, like it was coming toward you right from her mouth. But when she wasn't happy, you had to lean forward to hear her. I had to lean forward a lot after Ty left.

"He's got a good home, and he's got a good life," Reuben said. "If he don't want to be in it, it's because he's just dumb."

Bum. Come. Dumb. Fum. Gum. Hum. I didn't want to hear Reuben talk like that about Ty.

"He's living in a fantasy, a dream world," Reuben said.

"Reuben, the boy's all right," Mom said. "Ty is a

good, decent young man."

I wondered if Ty was living in a dream world. And if he was living in a dream world, did he know about dreams, like Mr. Moses knew about them? I was beginning to think a lot about the old man. I thought that I could be thinking about him because I didn't want to think about Ty or the little pieces of my life that seemed to go floating around the house. There was a warm feeling to Mr. Moses, a feeling that made me think he liked people a lot, maybe even liked me and Loren. It was good the way he talked to me and called me Mr. David. There were things I didn't know about him. He was probably too old to know good, even if he wasn't hundreds of years old the way he said he was. Him being that old didn't make any sense, but it didn't mess with me, not like Reuben's not making sense tightened my stomach.

I hated it when Reuben talked to himself. Ty said Reuben was crazy, and as soon as his crazy papers were filled out they were going to lock him up.

"So what do you want to do?" We were on the roof working on Sessi's house. She had made it bigger, six feet long and four feet wide, and high enough so that if I stood right in the middle, I could stand up almost straight, so it had to be at least five feet six inches.

"Why don't we go to the park and you can teach Kimi how to play basketball," Sessi said.

"It'll take too long to teach him," Loren said. "By the time he knows as much as me, he'll be too old to play."

"He doesn't have to be a professional," Sessi said. "He just wants to play an American game."

"You know anything about slavery?" I asked Sessi.

"Why do all Americans think Africans know so much about slavery?" Sessi asked. "We have the same books that you do."

"How come all Africans think that Americans know about basketball?" Loren said.

That was a good one and Sessi knew it. She fluttered her hands at us, really close to our faces. Sessi always did that, but Loren and I had both practiced not blinking.

"If Kimi wants to play ball with us tomorrow after church, he can come," I said.

I said I would pick Kimi up at two on Sunday; then Sessi said I should call her father and ask his permission before I came over. I told her that if I had to do all that asking for permission and everything, I would rather not take Kimi out. She gave me a cute smile and I knew I would do it anyway.

Loren and I were planning to go down to the Countee Cullen Library on 136th, but when I told him that Ty hadn't been home for two days, he said I should go to the pool hall on 141st Street.

"Sometimes he hangs out there," he said.

"How do you know that?"

"Me and Junebug went to that store next to it to buy some comic books, and we saw Ty with a guy wearing a red do-rag—he looked like a Blood or something."

"Ty?"

"No, the guy with the do-rag."

I asked Loren if he wanted to go to the pool hall with me, and he said he didn't care so we went down Malcolm X. When we got to 141st I stopped, and Loren pointed down the street where some guys were gathered in front of a store. It was almost to the next corner.

"You scared?" I asked him.

"Scared of what?"

I didn't know *of what* so I started walking again. Loren said we could go in and play some pool if we wanted to. I knew we weren't going to, and I could tell by the way Loren had his shoulders hunched up that he wasn't as brave as he was pretending.

One hundred forty-first Street is different from 145th. One hundred forty-fifth is wide and one of the main streets people use to get across town, so it's always crowded. Some of the buildings are new, and even the old ones are kept pretty clean. One hundred forty-first is quiet, and there are two empty lots on the block. Empty lots are like holes in the neighborhood.

Loren pointed out the pool hall, and I saw the older dudes just standing around on the sidewalk, like they were waiting for something to happen. It was hot but they were all wearing jackets. We stopped a little way down from them and I told Loren to look casual. What he did was to hunch his shoulders up even more.

"You going to go in?" he asked.

The pool hall on 141st Street is one of those places I didn't have to know a lot about to know I should stay away from it. I had passed its dark windows plenty of times and imagined what was going on inside.

I was just about to say no when I saw Ty coming out the door. He had on his black coat and baggy black pants. He looked around and started walking away from us. I nudged Loren, and we went after Ty.

My heart was beating fast, so I slapped my chest twice, the way Loren and I do to let each other know we're kind of nervous. Loren looked at me and then toward Ty.

"Ty!" I called to my brother as we got near him.

Ty turned around quickly, and I got the feeling he was ready to throw down if he had to. His coat was open and I could see his shirt was wrinkled and there was fuzzy stuff, it looked like cat hair, on the front of his pants. He smelled bad, too. Ty always stayed cleaned and neat. Now he looked and even smelled terrible.

"Yo, man, what you doing?"

"Hanging," I said. "What you doing?"

"Got some running to do," he said. "See you later tonight."

"You coming home?"

"Be in about midnight." Ty tilted his head back and

looked down his nose at me. "He giving you a hard time about me?"

I leaned my head back, the way he did, and said no. Ty told me to stay cool and keep Loren cool, too. Then he spun around and walked away.

"You should have asked him where he's been," Loren said after Ty had walked partway down the block.

"I was waiting for you to say something," I said.

"You think he's in some kind of trouble?" Loren asked.

"He doesn't like to be dirty," I said. "Something's wrong."

"If you want, you can send him to my office and I'll psychoanalyze him," Loren said.

"There's nothing like a good chat between a brother and a sister to set things right." Mr. Kerlin smiled and nodded. "Now, what we want is the same thing, to uplift the community. Am I right on that, my sister?"

"We're talking about the same thing," Mom said.

"Yes, we are," Mr. Kerlin said. "And there's no use in us fighting against each other when we are not the enemy. Indifference is the enemy. Apathy is the enemy."

"I'm sure you're anxious to improve the community," Mom said. She had on her hairdresser's apron and was leaning against the sink. "But your empty building has been one of the problems in the neighborhood for the past nine years."

"That is another area of agreement!" Mr. Kerlin held

his cigar between his fingers like it was a dart he was going to throw. "Now two factors have flowed together like two mighty rivers to create a tide of change. The first is the time. There's enough affluence in Harlem to make rehabilitating the building worthwhile. The second is need. As the city finally sees fit to pay some attention to the neglected areas, there arises a need for decent housing, and I am moved to provide some of that housing. Now, am I a bad man, Mrs. Curry?"

"And the fact that the city council was going to take over your *abandoned* building and give the Matthew Henson Community Project a grant to open a homeless shelter had nothing to do with your being moved?"

"I am genuinely hurt that you question a Christian's motives," Mr. Kerlin said. "I hope you believe that."

"Mr. Kerlin—"

"Call me Robert."

"Mr. Robert Kerlin," Mom said, and folded her hands across her chest, "you are a schemer and a scoundrel and the truth is not in you! Now that's what I believe."

"The Lord moves in mysterious ways. This I know," Mr. Kerlin said. "But deep in my heart I do believe that one day we will both look back on this day and these events and appreciate how we have uplifted One hundred forty-fifth Street. Uplifted the street and the community."

"I'm sure," Mom said.

"And we're giving meaningful employment to

neighborhood people," Mr. Kerlin said.

Mr. Kerlin looked pleased with himself as he swung his cigar around, and I knew Mom couldn't wait for him to leave. The way he was smiling and waving his cigar around, he was acting like it was his house and not ours.

Mom had gone in to wake my father up when Mr. Kerlin first came to the house, but he hadn't come out yet, and Mom left the kitchen and went into the bedroom again. I could hear her saying something about Mr. Kerlin's waiting for him, so I figured he must have been up and almost dressed.

"You sure are a fine young man." Mr. Kerlin was speaking to me.

"Thank you."

"Maybe one day you can be the superintendent of a big building, like your father." Mr. Kerlin put that cigar between his lips and turned it between his fingers.

"Maybe." He had forgotten about me being a pilot.

Reuben came out tucking his shirt into his pants. Mr. Kerlin started talking about how he needed him to fix up the rear door, the one that led out to the yard, because he thought someone had tried to break in. I noticed he didn't smile when he talked to Reuben. Before they left, Mom asked Reuben when he'd be home, and Mr. Kerlin said he would be a while.

"I don't see how Mr. Kerlin smokes them stinky cigars," I said after he had left.

"Loren's mother said that you saw Tyrone today," Mom said.

"We saw him down on One hundred forty-first Street."

Mom sat down and took a deep breath. "How did he look?" she asked.

"Not too cool," I said. "That's probably because he hasn't been changing his clothes. You know what I mean?"

"Yes, I know what you mean." Mom's voice got edgy. "Did he say anything about coming home?"

"He said he'd be by late tonight," I said.

"It would have been nice for you to let me know that you saw him," Mom said. "You knew I was worried about him, didn't you?"

"Yeah, but I didn't know if I should say anything in case he didn't come home," I said. "You'd just be worrying more."

Mom took my hand and kissed it, then she pulled me close and hugged me.

I was right. Ty didn't come home and he didn't call. I was awake most of the night, and Mom must have been awake as well. She came to the room twice and looked in, as if she might have missed him. I felt bad for me, but even worse for her.

When I got up in the morning, Mom was making soft-boiled eggs and toast. She answered good morning when I said it, but she said it low, the way she does when she doesn't want to talk a lot. I knew she had something on her mind, so I just waited for it to come out.

"You think your brother's using drugs?" she asked me.

Mom was holding her tea in front of her face and looking toward the window. She rolled her eyes toward me and asked again.

"I don't know for sure," I said, "but I don't think so."

"Is that because you don't see any signs?" she asked. "Or is it just because he's your brother and you love him so much that . . ."

She was crying again and I put my hand on hers. She got out a little smile and took my hand. She was quiet for a long minute, maybe two.

"Lord Jesus, give us strength," she said. "Give us strength."

I helped do the dishes and we started downstairs. Mom had to go to the Bronx to take her aunt Mabel to the doctor, and I thought I would go over to Loren's house. On the way down we met Reuben coming upstairs carrying a brown paper bag. I hadn't even thought about him not being home.

"Come on up and have some donuts and coffee," he said. His breath smelled bad. Whiskey.

Mom told him about having to take Mabel to the doctor, that she had an inner ear infection and was always in danger of falling down. Reuben looked mad. His jaw tightened up and I didn't know what he was going to do. He told me to come upstairs and have some breakfast with him.

"I'm going to Loren's house," I said.

He grabbed me by the collar and threw me against the stairs.

"Reuben!" Mom put herself over me. "I'll call Mabel and tell her I can't come."

"Go on! Go on! What do I care?" He was shouting. "You said you was going to take her to the doctor, so go on! I'm finished working. Me and David are going to have some donuts and milk, and then he can go see his friend."

"Reuben, please be careful." She moved toward me, and Reuben pushed her away.

"I'm okay, Mom," I said. "I'm okay."

Reuben was helping me up, and I was trying hard not to cry. I knew that would just make him madder.

"Go on, woman!" he said to Mom. "We'll be okay."

I started up the stairs as Mom started down. I didn't look back at her.

"I was born one year, almost to the day, that Malcolm X died," Reuben said. There was sugar on his chin from the donut he was eating. "They had to kill Malcolm because they couldn't control him. You know they can control most people. Did you know that?"

"How?"

"They do it by making you think in circles," Reuben said. "See, if they tell you to do something you don't want to do, right away you're going to think they're stupid and you won't do it. Say a man walks up to you and tells you to give him your money. What are you going to say?"

"Probably no," I said.

"That's just what you're going to say," Reuben said. "But if he told you there were germs on your money, you'd give him a look and wonder what his game is. Then you'd wonder why he's coming up to you. So your thinking went to the money, then to him, and then circled right back to you. See what I mean?"

"Yeah."

"That's how they control you," Reuben said. "They talk about you giving up your money, then they talk about the money having germs on it, and before you know it, your money's gone."

"Nobody said my money had germs on it," I said.

"No, but they're telling you that it's better to use a credit card instead of carrying money around, don't they?"

"That's so nobody will rob you," I said.

"No, that's so you won't think your money's going," Reuben said. "You buy something with a credit card and you take it out of your pocket. The man zips it through his machine, and then you put it back in your pocket. You got your TV, your CD, whatever, and you still got your credit card in your pocket. You think you got everything, but your money's gone. See what I mean?"

"Yes." I didn't know what he meant, but I didn't want to say that.

The telephone rang and Reuben answered it. It was Aunt Mabel wanting to know if Mom was on her way. Reuben told her yes. Then he hung up and sat back down.

There had been six donuts in the bag. Reuben had

eaten one and I had eaten one. Now he pushed another one to me across the table.

"Another way they control you is through your dreaming. When you go to sleep at night, you got to dream or you go crazy. Even dogs dream. You ever see a dog dream?"

"Yeah, my friend Ralph had a dog," I said. "And you could tell he was dreaming about running because his legs would go like he was running and so would his tail."

"They put things on TV, real pretty things, and get you to dreaming about them," Reuben said. "You see them on television when they come on, but you just push them on out of your mind because they ain't real to you. You know what I mean?"

"I think so."

"They put a house on TV, all spotless and shiny. The wife, she's smiling, the children are smiling, everything is pretty and nice. Maybe they even give them a little problem so they look like a real family. Looking for a new car—something like that. Then they go back to the news or the weather but that little scene, the house and family and all, is still in your head. You think you got it pushed out, but it's just out of the front of your mind and pushed down into your sub-conscious mind and you dream about it. They got you dreaming about what they want you to dream about, so they're controlling you."

"Oh."

He kept on talking about how people were trying to control him, and I was getting a little scared. He said Mom was trying to control him too.

"Who is supposed to be the man of the family?" he asked.

"You are."

"Now if I'm supposed to be the man of the family and she's standing up against me, then we're fighting about who the man is," he said. "She's keeping me off balance. Just like you're playing ball and somebody tries to go around you. They move this way and that way and you're trying to follow them, and if you lose your balance they go around you. You don't have to lose it big-time, just a little, and they're gone. Then, if they don't want to go around you, if all they want to do is control you, they act like they're going around you but then they don't go. That's what she's doing. Yeah."

He looked like he was getting mad. I tried to act like I wasn't scared or anything.

The faster Reuben talked, the more donuts he ate. He finished them all and then he said he had to clean the bathroom. He told me I could go over to Loren's house if I wanted.

I wondered what kinds of dreams Reuben had. When I thought about him dreaming, I thought of him having a storm in his head, with lightning and far-off thunder and the wind blowing big raindrops in your face and a bigger storm coming just down the street, just around the corner, like a monster waiting for you. I thought Reuben dreamed of monsters that scared him.

They scared me, too.

Me and Loren took Kimi and Sessi over to the park. We tried to teach Kimi how to play basketball, but all he wanted to do was to write down the rules in a notebook he brought with him. Sessi liked the game, and every time she threw the ball toward the basket, she jumped up and down and clapped her hands. I enjoyed watching her and Kimi, and even the way Loren was enjoying himself.

"Hey, man, you're laughing again," Loren said. "You're looking like the old David now."

We played two games, with me and Kimi on one side and Loren and Sessi on the other, and after a while we were all laughing and just fooling around. When Sessi said she and Kimi had to go home, I was sorry. Loren said he had to go too, and I decided just to sit in the park for a while.

"I'll e-mail you," Loren said.

I watched my three friends walk off, with Kimi trying to dribble by slapping at the ball. As happy as I had been with them, I was sad as they left. I didn't want to go home. What had Mr. Moses said? There weren't any homeless people, just people not in their homes.

I was thinking a lot about Ty and wondering how he was feeling. Was he wondering what me and Mom were doing? Or maybe about his bed? Maybe he would be thinking about his comics, if I was messing with them or just reading them. Maybe he was thinking about Reuben and about being hit. Nobody likes to think about being hit.

I saw Mr. Moses coming across the playground, sort of shuffling from side to side, wearing too many clothes for such a hot day. He was pushing a shopping cart filled with old clothes and newspapers. There were times I liked to hear him talking, but there were times I liked to be alone with my thoughts, to let them sit in my head and just get the feel of them through me without being disturbed.

He stopped a few feet away from me and, for a moment, stood perfectly still.

"Hello," I said.

"Sometimes . . ."

"I don't want to talk to you," I said.

"Sometimes when it hurts so much, we want to bury

the pain deep inside of us," the old man said.

"I don't want to talk to you," I said again. "Why don't you just go somewhere?" All I wanted to do was to sit on the park bench and be by myself. I didn't want to talk to Mr. Moses, or even to Loren.

"You just tell me why you can't stand to hear me talking, so I can take that away with me," Mr. Moses said.

"I'm tired of people talking to me. Talking doesn't do any good anyway. It's just about people laying their stuff on you, trying to make you agree with them."

"Yeah, well, that's true. That's true. But we only got one way of seeing the world, and we all running around trying to get everybody to see what we see," he said. "You can't blame a man for that."

"Yes, you can," I said.

"I guess you don't want to hear another of my dreams?" he said. "It's a good one, nothing bad happens in it."

"No."

"It's about me working in the field down in South Carolina, about two hundred and fifteen years ago. You ain't never seen a field this big. Well, in this dream it was a hot day, so hot you could reach out and grab the heat in your hand. I had done got into a beef with one of the other fellows in the field. I don't know what it was about, some little thing." Mr. Moses put his fingertips together in front of him. "Anyway, I seen him in the field a little ahead of me two rows down. He seen me, too, and started picking faster and moving on down his row. Then I started picking faster to keep up with him. Before long we was snatching cotton like two fools under that hot sun.

"The old overseer seen us, and he knew we needed to be picking all day and wasn't going to do it like that. He snapped his whip to let us know he was watching us. I heard that whip snap but I just dropped my head and kept on picking as fast as I could.

"I walked and walked and picked and picked. And the spot on my shoulder, the spot where that bag went across my body, got so hot, I thought I could feel it burning through my body. I looked up at the other fellow and he was doing the same and we was both suffering for it. Lord knows we was both suffering, but we had got caught up in it and couldn't do nothing about it. Now ain't that a sorry dream? Two men couldn't find no way out the pain. Ain't that a sorry dream?"

"That don't sound like much of a dream to me," I said.

"I didn't say it was going to be a fancy dream," he said. "I just said it was going to be a dream."

"Dreams don't mean anything anyway," I said. "They're just thoughts that run through your head. Your dreams aren't even interesting. Anyway, I think you read them in a book about slavery or something. You talking about picking cotton and whips and all that stuff, it probably came straight from a book."

"I don't know, maybe you're right," Mr. Moses said. He had got to the bench and, putting one hand on the back of it, had eased himself down to a sitting position. "On the other hand, dreams might be the only things we got that's real. After the wind has lifted up what's left of the body and sent it swirling into the distance, and all the memories that seemed to be our lives have yellowed and faded away, then all that's left of a life is the footprints the dreams left behind."

"I don't want to be rude or nothing, but . . . why don't you just leave or something?" I said.

"Yes, I see it's time to leave you to yourself," Mr. Moses said. "But let me remind you of something you need to know. It is not only the wicked that travel with pain. Sometimes it is the innocent as well."

He stood up and started picking up his things. He turned his shopping cart around and started pushing it away.

"You can stay," I said when I saw him going, but the words didn't come out too loud and he kept on walking.

I felt bad when Mr. Moses left, and a little surprised how easily the words had come from me that had pushed him away.

Two boys I knew came into the playground. One was Scotty, who lived in the projects. He was okay, but the other one was Robert Davis, and he was always starting something. I got up and started walking toward the gate.

"Hey, punk, you got any money?" Robert said.

I didn't say anything, and Robert came over and pushed my shoulder. I turned to him and just looked at him. He tried to put on a mean face but I wasn't going for it. If he wanted to fight me I was ready, even if I was sure I was going to lose. Scotty called to him to come on and play some one-on-one. Robert called me a punk again, but he went on and played with Scotty. I wondered what kind of stupid dreams he would have.

Ty came home in the middle of the day. He took a long shower and then fell across the bed.

"You look tired," I said.

"I am tired," he said.

"Mom was worried that you were using drugs or something," I said.

"What's that supposed to be, the magic word? *Drugs?* Anything happens in the streets and the only thing people can think of is drugs. You can have some kind of . . . some kind of disease or something and people still talking about drugs," Ty said. "I'm just busy and she's not used to busy people. You want to get paid out there on the street, you have to be busy."

We heard the outside door open and shut, and

Reuben's heavy step in the hallway. I looked over at Ty. He sat up, took the remote, and put on the television. Reuben came to the door and just looked at Ty for a while.

"Glad to see you home, boy."

Ty did a little lame nod of his head and I saw Reuben's jaw get tight. The phone rang and I said I would get it.

Loren was on the phone, all excited, saying that Mom was on television. He told me what channel to get.

I ran into the living room. "Mom's on television!" I called.

Reuben came in just as the picture of Mom came on.

"Turn up the sound!" he said.

"I still believe in the project," Mom was saying. She looked fat on television. "I just feel that my personal commitments make me more needed elsewhere."

"I understand that your husband is part of the opposition," a man's voice was saying. "Is that why you're dropping out of the controversy, and is the community that torn up about the Matthew Henson shelter?"

"The community's not torn up," Mom said, shaking her head. "There are different opinions of how to use the neighborhood resources, that's all."

"She sounds like a real television reporter," Ty said.

"Is gentrification an issue?" the reporter asked.

"No, gentrification is not an issue," Mom said.

"What's that?" I asked as Mom turned and walked away.

Reuben held up his hand for me to keep quiet.

"Today's question is how to use the precious resources of Harlem." The camera pulled back and the black reporter looked very serious. "And it's also a matter of who exactly will benefit from the enormous amount of money now circulating in this up-and-coming community. For Channel Sixty-three News, this is Mike Grimmett, from the Upper West Side."

"She looked like herself but a little different," I said. "I liked it."

The phone rang again and it was Loren asking me if I had seen Mom, and I told him yes. He said she looked foxy and I told him he'd better watch his mouth.

"So I guess you won," Tyrone said to Reuben.

"You have to do what you have to do," Reuben said. "You want to go to the park and play some ball?"

"Who? Me?" Tyrone looked at Reuben like he was crazy or something.

"What you think, I can't play ball?"

"Yeah, well, maybe some other time," Ty said.

"You think I can't play ball?"

"What you going to do, lay in some father-son time?" Ty asked.

This funny look came on Reuben's face, like he was hurt or something. "I just wondered if you was man enough to play ball," he said.

"I'm as much man as I got to be," Ty said.

Ty wasn't all that good. The big kids who were good

could take him easy. He thought he was good, though, but I knew he shouldn't play against Reuben. I think in Ty's heart he knew better, but something was eating at him. I called Loren and asked him if could come to the park, and he said yes.

By the time Ty got dressed and we walked downstairs, Loren was already on the stoop waiting for us.

"Your mom said you could come?" I asked.

"She's not home," Loren said. "My father's not home either."

"You're going to get one of those all-night lectures about how kids end up in jail," I said.

"When I tell her your mother was on television, she's going to forget the lecture," Loren said.

We got to the park and I got a ball from the park man. Reuben wanted a jump ball, but Ty told him to take it out.

Mr. Moses was on the bench and I thought he was sleeping, but then he waved, and me and Loren waved back.

Reuben took the ball out and started backing into the basket. Ty got behind him and was trying to hold him out of the lane, but there was no way he was going to hold Reuben out when he could hardly keep me out.

Reuben backed Ty all the way in and then did a little turnaround layup that went in. Ty got the ball, and right away he started a lot of head shaking, like he was going to fake somebody out. I looked at Reuben, and he looked the same way he did when he was mad at me. I could see all the muscles in his neck. He's got a lot of muscles and I knew he was strong. Ty couldn't back him into the lane, and then he tried to put a move on him but he still couldn't get past. Finally Ty threw up a jump shot that didn't even touch the backboard.

They were supposed to play until one of them got to ten, and I knew who that was going to be. Me and Loren sat on the bench.

"Ty doesn't have a chance," Loren said.

I was hoping that Ty didn't mouth off and get Reuben mad. Sometimes I didn't like what Ty did, but I hated it when him and Reuben got into it. I especially didn't want Loren to see Reuben hit Ty.

They played until the score was six to nothing and then Ty quit.

"You hacking me to death!" he said.

"You didn't think I could play ball, did you?"

Ty just walked away, and Reuben told him to come back but Ty kept walking. Then Reuben went after him and put his arm around Ty's neck. It looked like they were just talking when they came back, but I knew better. Reuben was mad again. They played for two more points with Ty hardly trying, and then Reuben asked him if he gave up.

"Yeah." Ty was mad because Reuben has a way of making you feel little inside. Ty didn't even look over to where me and Loren were sitting.

Reuben threw me the ball and told me to take it back to the park house, and Loren asked me if I wanted to play some one-on-one. I said I had to go home, but I took a shot before I left.

Just then Mr. Moses started coughing. He was coughing bad, like his whole body was going back and forth.

"I'll get some water!" Loren said.

The park was suddenly like a bunch of scenes, all drifting away from the basketball court. Ty, in the same black coat he always wears, was walking across the playground with his head down. Loren was running to the park house to get some water, and Reuben was standing near the foul line looking at Mr. Moses coughing.

"He's sick," I said.

"Stay away from him," Reuben said.

"No, he's okay," I said. "We know him. He's a nice guy. We should try to help him."

"You need to stay away from people like that," Reuben said. "They ain't got nothing for you. They're just dead people waiting for a place to lay down."

Loren came back with the water and gave it to Mr. Moses, and he drank it and stopped coughing.

"Let's go," Reuben called to me.

"We should see if he's okay," I said.

"I said let's go!" Reuben's voice was angry.

"I feel bad about not helping Mr. Moses," I called to Reuben. I could feel my eyes tearing up. "Real bad."

I didn't look at Mr. Moses when we were leaving

because I felt so bad. I didn't even get the water. Loren got it and gave it to him. Just as we got to the gate, Mrs. Hart came jogging up.

"David's mother was on television," Loren said.

Mrs. Hart had this little smile on her face and looked at Reuben, and then at me, and then back at Reuben and asked him if everything was all right.

"Yeah, she was just on the news," Reuben said.

I looked over at Loren and he had this real calm look on his face, and I knew he was going to make up a lot of stuff to tell his mom. Loren's mom said he had to go to the store with her, and they went off.

Me and Reuben walked home together. I hardly ever walked anywhere with Reuben, and all the way home I felt that my legs were stiff. It was a funny feeling.

Mom was home and Reuben said he had seen her on television.

"I thought it was time for me to withdraw from the project," she said.

"Do what you want," Reuben said.

I went into the room and saw Ty lying across the bed, and that made me feel good. I sat next to him and rubbed his shoulder a little. He slapped my hand away without turning, but then he saw it was me and gave me a little punch, the way he does sometimes.

"You feel messed around?" I asked.

"He was hacking me to death," Ty said. "That's all he can do is hack somebody to death."

"I'm glad you're home," I said.

"I owe some guys a lot of money," he said. "Four Bennies."

"Why you owe them four hundred dollars?"

Ty touched his head with his finger. "Stupid," he said. "Just plain old stupid."

"When you got to pay them?"

"Yesterday."

We were having spaghetti and meatballs for dinner, and I asked if Loren could come over. Mom said to ask Reuben and he said it was okay with him. Loren loves spaghetti and meatballs.

When I sat back down after calling him and telling Mom that he was coming, Reuben said that me and Loren were really good friends.

"You ever go to his house to eat?" he said.

"I don't like what his mother makes," I said.

"You and him need to stay away from these bums on the street," Reuben said. "You never know what they up to. They can have some kind of disease, they can be up to no good, you can't tell."

"Who's this?" Mom was putting olive oil in the sauce.

"We met this man who says he's three hundred years old," I said. "He said he keeps dreams and carries them around with him for all that time."

"Stay away from him!" Reuben said.

"Why?"

"Because I said so."

"I think he's okay," I said.

"Stay away from him!"

The tears came again and I just let them run down my face. Reuben was looking at me, and he was mad, and for the first time in my life I didn't look away from him.

I was sorry when Loren came over. Reuben sat with us at the dinner table, and nobody said anything as we ate. At first it could have been that nobody had anything to say, but then we all knew how quiet we were being, and it was like we were caught up in it.

Mr. Moses' dream came to mind, and I imagined him in the cotton field, in the hot sun, caught up in his dream. But he hadn't told me why they had been picking the cotton so fast. That was a part of the dream that didn't make any sense. Having a hard time swallowing spaghetti didn't make sense, either.

Mom got a letter from my school saying I had been recommended for a scholarship to a private school in Riverdale. She was happy about it and said I would love it.

"I don't want to go to a private school," I said.

"How do you know?" Mom asked. "They're asking us to drop by this afternoon. We should at least go and listen to what the program has to offer."

I didn't want to change schools. I liked Frederick Douglass Academy, my school, and, more than that, I liked my friends there.

My school is only a few blocks from where I live, so we walked. On the way over Mom asked me about the man I had met in the park. I told her he was just an old man who had told me about his dreams.

"He ever touch you?" she asked, putting a smile in her voice.

"No," I said. "He's not weird."

"You understand why your father was concerned?"

"I didn't understand why he was so mad," I said. "I don't understand why he's always mad."

"He's got problems," Mom said. "And sometimes his problems are hard to understand."

"You understand them?"

"Not all the time," she said.

"Mr. Moses, that's the old man, said that people get mad in layers, and then all the layers get mixed up and they act strange."

"Sometimes people . . . That might make sense, but because one thing makes sense doesn't mean the man is all right. I don't want to say he's bad or anything, but I think we have to be careful."

There was a group of nuns standing on the sidewalk at 148th Street. They were wearing blue dresses and little white caps. I liked the way they looked, standing together on the corner waiting for the light to change. "I wonder if they would think he's bad or good?"

"They haven't met him," Mom said.

"Neither have you."

"You're very smart, young man," Mom said, "but I know a little more about the ways of the world than you do."

"You understand Ty's problems?"

"Ty is a young man dealing with adolescence," she answered. "He needs to move into manhood, and that involves a lot of decisions and a lot of soul-searching. He needs to discover who he really is and what he really wants to become."

"He owes some people four hundred dollars," I said.

Mom stopped walking. We were in front of the Chinese take-out place. "How do you know that?" she asked.

"He told me. I think when he didn't come home those days, he was hiding from them."

"Is he involved in drugs?"

"I don't know."

"What do you mean you don't know?" Her face got mad and she was yelling. "You see him every day! You sleep in the same room! You—you—"

"I just don't know!" I said.

She was crying. She put her hand to her face and then took it away again.

"Evelyn, how are you?" It was a woman from the church. A tall, thin woman, she had on a floppy white hat. She wore a big silver cross that hung on the outside of her dress. She looked at Mom and then at me. "Is everything all right?"

"Everything's fine," Mom said. "It's just been one of those days. How've you been?"

"Blessed!" the woman said. "Just remember, the Lord not only answers prayer but he's always listening!"

"I'll remember that," Mom said.

The woman walked on down the block, and Mom took me by the hand and into the Chinese place. We sat down and Mom asked the girl cleaning tables for two sodas. The girl nodded and went behind the counter to get the sodas.

"Sometimes people can get hurt over money," Mom said. "And four hundred dollars is a lot of money for a seventeen-year-old to be owing. I can get the money if it's necessary. I would love to know anything you know about it. Why do you think he was hiding from these people? Are they gang people?"

"I don't know."

"Then how do you know he owes anybody money?" Mom asked.

The girl brought the sodas over and put them down on the table. Mom didn't say anything until she had left. Then she asked again how I knew Ty owed the $400.

"I saw he was upset, and so I asked him," I said.

Mom was crying again, and I felt sorry for her. In a way I was sorry I had told her about the money. Maybe Ty was involved in drugs and maybe he wasn't. He didn't tell me everything. That's the way Ty is mostly, keeping things to himself. I didn't think he had anybody he would call a best friend.

We drank the sodas, paid for them, and then went to the school. The guard opened the door, and we signed in and went up to the second floor where the offices were. Mrs. Finley, my English teacher, was there and said hello.

While we waited for Mr. Weinstein, Mom asked me if Reuben knew about the $400, and I said that I didn't think so.

"We have to look at this as a family," she said. "We'll have to sit down with Ty, and with your father, and decide what to do."

"If Ty is scared, we'd better get the money," I said.

"I can't do it without . . ." She stopped for a while. "Do you think we should tell your father?"

"I don't know."

I thought about Reuben sitting at the kitchen table, with all his little bits of anger buzzing like flies around his head. There was no way I wanted to tell him that Ty owed somebody a lot of money, but I didn't want Ty to be in trouble, either. Loren was my absolute best friend, but sometimes Ty did things that made me feel real good about him. Once I got a 90 on a paper and it was on the kitchen table, and he picked it up and looked at it while he was talking on the phone. When he finished talking, he took a pencil out, crossed out the 90, and put a 100 on it. That made me feel real good.

When we got into Mr. Weinstein's office, he told us how lucky I was to be recommended for the program. The conversation went on and on, but all I was thinking was that I didn't want to be there and I knew Mom was thinking about Ty. We ended up telling Mr. Weinstein that we would think about it. I could see he was disappointed.

When we got home, Ty wasn't there and Reuben was asleep. There was an empty beer bottle on the table, and Mom put it in the garbage under the sink.

"I'm going to tell Tyrone that we'll get the money for him somehow," Mom said. "If he tells you anything more about it, will you let me know?"

"Yeah, I guess."

"David, it's not like telling on someone," Mom said. "Sometimes it's necessary to bring everything into the open so that we can deal with the problems as a family. David, I need you to help me. Can you understand that?"

I said yes, that I could understand it, but it wasn't all that easy. It seemed that at the beginning of summer I just had to go from day to day, without a lot of things to think about. Everything had a place, and a shape, and a time to happen. In the mornings the sun came up, and when I looked out the window, I could see 145ᵗʰ Street stirring itself awake and listen to the morning sounds of cars and buses and kids playing. Then I would see Loren and maybe go to the park, and it would always be there. Mom would come into the kitchen smiling, and Ty would float through the house being Ty. Even Reuben, when he was acting strange, seemed to move in his own space, not touching the world me and Loren lived in. That wasn't good, but I could just observe it, the way I thought I would observe China if I ever had the chance to see it, or some other foreign country with a landscape that was totally different from Harlem. But now the need to understand everything was creeping up on me. People who at one time were just around now needed to be fitted into a picture that kept changing as I tried to bring the pieces together.

Ty got home late, and he woke me up. He asked me why I had told Mom that he owed somebody $400.

"I just did," I said.

"You better keep your mouth out of my business," he said.

Ty saying that made me so mad, I felt like hitting him. As I listened to him undressing and opening the window to let some air into the room, I thought about me and him having a fight and me winning. I didn't want to hurt him, just to let him know how mad I was. And then I thought of Reuben getting mad and hitting Ty, and I knew I didn't want to fight Ty, or anyone.

Saturday morning. I called Loren to see what he wanted to do. He said he wanted to go to the movies. One thing about Loren was that he could always get the money he needed to do something.

"Hang around for a while," I said. "Maybe I can get the money to go with you. You want to go to the Magic?"

"Yep."

Magic Johnson's theater is six dollars on Saturday morning. I had two dollars and thirty cents, which was pretty good, but I wasn't sure if I should ask Mom or Reuben. Mom was happy about the school thing, but Reuben was mad about it because she opened the letter. She should have let him do it, but I wouldn't have wanted him to if it was bad. You could never tell about Reuben.

I e-mailed Loren and told him how much I had and asked him what was playing. Two minutes later his mom called and said that I needed three dollars and seventy cents more and she didn't know what was playing. She said that she thought that Loren was with me. I don't know how Mrs. Hart got Loren's e-mail password. I sent him another e-mail on his superhero address. I was glad she didn't know that one—at least she didn't answer it.

Ty was still in bed. I heard somebody in the kitchen and went out to see who it was. Reuben.

He didn't say anything, just sat and looked down as if he was looking into his coffee cup, but I knew he wasn't seeing it. He was thinking about something. I wondered what his thinking was like. When I thought about something, it was like remembering things that had happened, or imagining things that might happen. Sometimes I could remember feelings. But when Reuben was thinking, when he was sitting at the table with the fingers of one hand over the other one, what he was thinking made the muscles in his arms move, and sometimes his shoulders would jerk forward. When I was there with him, when he thought I might have seen him, he would look up at me, and I would sit still and pretend I hadn't seen it. But the two of us would be sitting there, not moving, me not even breathing hardly, and he would know he was in my mind.

I had never been in the room with him when he sat

alone in the darkness and called out. I was glad I was not in the darkness with him.

The phone rang twice and I heard Mom answer it. She came out of the bedroom in her housecoat and slippers and said that Loren was on the phone. I picked up the receiver in the kitchen, already thinking about the movie.

"Hey, Loren!"

"Hey, David!" Loren answered. "Guess what happened?"

"What?"

"Me, Sessi, and Kimi found Mr. Moses laying out in the park," Loren said. "I thought he was dead, but he was just sick."

"What did you do?"

"The park man wasn't there, so we went to Sessi's house and told her mom and she made some food for him, and we took it to the park and gave it to him," Loren said. "Man, he's real sick."

"So what you going to do?"

"I don't know," Loren answered. "Sessi said he should go to the hospital, but he don't want to go."

"Was he drunk?"

"No, but he's got that kind of bad smell old people get," Loren said. "He's still sitting out there on the park bench. You know, just a little way in from the front of the park where the water fountain is."

"You think he's got any money for medicine?"

"He probably doesn't even use medicine," Loren said. "He probably uses roots and stuff like that."

"Where are you now?"

"Home," Loren said. "Where are you?"

"I'm—I'm home because that's where you called," I said. "I'm going to go see if I can go out. Can you come out again?"

"No."

"What did Sessi's mom make for him?"

"Some soup, I think," Loren said. "It smelled like African food."

I told Loren I would call him later and hung up. Then I asked Mom if I could go out and see about Mr. Moses. She said maybe it wasn't such a good idea. She glanced over at Reuben.

He looked up at me. He didn't say anything, just looked at me.

"Loren called and said Mr. Moses was sick in the park," I said. "I want to go and see if I can help him."

"That's that old man?" His voice was calm.

"Yes."

"No," Reuben said.

If I felt bad before, I felt even worse.

"If somebody is sick and I just don't care about it, I think that's wrong," I said.

"David, why don't you go to your room," Mom said.

"Who is this guy, anyway?" Reuben's voice got loud. "How do I know who this man is?"

"He's just an old man," I said.

"What did he say to you?"

"He said he keeps dreams," I said. "He said he's got dreams that are, like, hundreds of years old. He remembers them and then one day he's going to pass them on to somebody else. He asked me if I wanted to keep them."

"You need to stay away from strangers," Reuben said. "Didn't your mom ever tell you that?"

"Will you help him?"

Reuben twisted away hard. He turned his head and looked at me over his shoulder. He was breathing hard.

"Sessi's mother gave him some food and he ate it," I said.

"Go on to your room!" Reuben's voice was getting louder. Mom came over and started pushing me out of the room.

"We could make him some tea," I said.

Reuben jumped up and came toward me and I closed my eyes. Mom grabbed me and was yelling at Reuben not to hit me. She was yelling and hanging on to me, and I had my eyes closed as tight as I could get them and was waiting for him to hit me.

I could hear him breathing and was hoping he had taken his pills. I thought about him hitting his hand against the wall one time until his knuckles were bleeding.

"Get your coat on!" Reuben was saying. "I'll go see him! I'll go see him!"

Mom told Reuben that he didn't have to go, that the old man would be all right, but he was upset and I knew he wasn't listening.

I put my sweater on and we went downstairs together. All the time, he was talking, saying how he had to go to work and he didn't have time to mess with no old crazy men.

It had rained and there were puddles everywhere. I stepped in one and splashed a little water on Reuben, but he didn't say anything. He was walking fast. I almost had to run to keep up with him. We went up the hill to the park, and I saw Mr. Moses sitting on the bench. Reuben slowed down, then stopped a few feet away from Mr. Moses and started staring at him.

Mr. Moses looked smaller than he had before, and his head was slumped down against his chest. His chest was rising and falling slowly, and I thought he was either asleep or real sick. I wanted to tell Reuben that we could go. Then he looked up and saw us. He raised his hand, like he was trying to wave to us. The nails on his hand were chipped and yellow against his dark skin. He nodded and spoke softly. Maybe he had said my name, but I couldn't hear it clearly.

I sat down next to him. "You okay?"

"These old bones are like a great rock in a weary land," Mr. Moses said. "But I keep rolling on."

"You need some medicine or something?" Reuben asked.

Mr. Moses looked up. "I'm all right, son," he said. "I thank you for coming out to see about me."

Reuben's shoulders had been hunched up, and he relaxed them a little. Then he sat down on the other side of Mr. Moses.

There were a few drops of rain and a little breeze, but it wasn't too cold. Right on the walkway, where the path met the dirt, there was a worm. A sparrow was picking up crumbs not far off from it, and I was wondering if it was going to eat the worm.

"You been to a doctor?" Reuben asked, looking down at the ground.

"I'll be okay," Mr. Moses said. "Sometimes the tiredness just sneaks up on me and catches me with my back turned. I'll be okay."

"I got a place you can stay if you need it." Reuben leaned back against the park bench. "Ain't nothing permanent, but you can sleep there for a few days if you don't bother nothing."

"I got a place to stay," Mr. Moses said, "but I appreciate what you're saying. Appreciate it right along."

"It's getting late." Reuben started to stand. "If you don't need nothing, I might as well get to work."

"The other night I dreamed about something that happened a long time ago," Mr. Moses said, "down in Georgia, about a mile off where you turn to head toward Athens. . . ."

"Those dreams of yours are for kids," Reuben said. "I don't want to hear them."

Mr. Moses turned and looked up at Reuben, and they were just looking at each other, Reuben looking mad and Mr. Moses looking like he was trying to see what was in Reuben's face.

"There was two mens, a stocky old boy named Ed Johnson and his best friend, Cammie Washington." Mr. Moses continued with his story, speaking very softly. "Cammie spelled his last name just like the president did. Anyway, a white farmer who was a deacon at that church claimed he was in his bed when somebody broke in his house and beat him up and took the money from the church services. He said he didn't rightly know who it was except it was a black man.

"The sheriff deputized some fellows and they got all of us, including Cammie and Ed Johnson, and lined us all up in the street so the farmer could take a good look at us. He went down the line and couldn't pick out nobody for sure. Then the sheriff asked who it might have been even if he wasn't sure, and he still couldn't pick out anybody for sure but said the robber could have favored Cammie. That's all that sheriff needed. He locked up Cammie and wasn't listening to nothing that was going to turn him away. By the time the case came up before the judge two weeks later, the farmer was saying he was pretty sure it was Cammie.

"Now that didn't mean nothing to us black folks, because we knew it didn't matter if Cammie had done it or not. If they wanted to find you guilty, you was guilty."

"Is this a dream or a story?" Reuben asked.

"I'm telling you the story, then I'm going to tell you the dream," Mr. Moses said. "The story went on that Cammie got sentenced to serve three years, but that didn't satisfy everybody in the town because there had been a lot of back-and-forth between the blacks and the whites. Then some folks decided they needed to teach us all a lesson by lynching Cammie.

"The night they took Cammie out the jail we was all scared. Cammie was calling out for mercy and saying the farmer knew it wasn't him, that he was a Christian man. They rounded up about nine of us and made us come into the middle of town, Iris Street, where they were holding Cammie. They put him up on a Model T Ford, tied his legs together, and put a rope around his neck. There was a general store on the corner, and some of them was drinking soda from bottles they had bought.

"They all had guns—shotguns, pistols, rifles. There wasn't nothing we could do about it but stand there and watch the whole thing. Cammie, he commenced to praying and calling out to his wife to take care of his kids. It was a pitiful sight, but not pitiful enough to move the cold hearts that was gathered there that night.

"After the hanging the white folks drifted off, and some of the black folks stayed to help take Cammie down. Then somebody said that Ed Johnson might have had a stroke because he couldn't move. I went over to Ed and seen something that I will never forget all my life, and which I dream about all the time. All the time. Ed was naturally a coal-dark black man, but he had lost his color. He looked gray, and ashy. 'Moses, help me, I can't move.' That's what he said. You could see he was struggling to take a step, but nothing happened."

I was hoping that Mr. Moses would stop his story, but he didn't.

"We got Cammie down and took him to the Free Will Baptist Colored Church, and some of the sisters stayed there with Cammie's wife through the night," Mr. Moses said. "Then we had to take Ed Johnson home. We got him home and laid him down on his bed. He begged us to stay with him. Just tarry awhile, he asked. But we were all upset about Cammie dying and we had our own families to take care of. I looked back at Ed in that bed, and something told me to go back and see to him. He looked cold, like somebody fixing to pass the vale, and I thought that if I had a blanket, if I could have got him warm, maybe he would have got his strength back. Ed Johnson didn't get out of that bed but one time for the next three months, and that was when he died and they carried him out. He had lost all his strength— he didn't have no more nature in him than a dead man."

"What you about, man? Scaring kids with your stupid stories?" The veins in Reuben's neck were swelling. "Why don't you just shut that mess up?"

"Man is scared by dreams and terrified by visions," Mr. Moses' voice rose and quivered as he spoke. "And when I dream this dream, of men in a great circle, watching death grinning in their midst, and their strength falling away like the leaves of autumn, I *am* scared."

"Please, Mr. Moses, please stop!" I said. "Please stop!"

"Go on home with your father, David." Mr. Moses spoke softly. "It's getting dark."

The dream Mr. Moses told us scared me. My hand was shaking when I stood up. Reuben started off and I started to say good-bye to Mr. Moses, but I could only wave.

I ran until I caught up with Reuben, and we walked home together. He began to say bad things about Mr. Moses. He said that he should die. I wanted to ask him if he was scared, because he sounded as scared as I was, but I didn't. I knew it would have made him even madder.

We got home and Mama was sitting on the edge of the couch. She looked from me to Reuben and back at me, the way she always does. Then she asked me how my friend was.

"I think he'll be okay," I said.

"Tell your mother what that fool was saying," Reuben said.

"He said he dreams about a man who saw his best friend lynched," I said. "And then he lost all of his strength and couldn't get out of bed."

"If you don't have a disease, you don't lose your strength," Reuben said. "That old man's never read a science book. If he can read at all."

"It sounds a little like your friend— What's his name?"

"Mr. Moses."

"It sounds like Mr. Moses might be worried about his own strength," Mama said. "And you have to remember that old people sometimes get a little confused about what they're thinking, especially if they're a little sick. Your friend can be worried about dying, and that's what he's actually thinking about."

I didn't think he was talking about himself. I thought he was talking about his dreams, but I wasn't sure what the difference was. It was like the dreams went along and became part of his life, and his life became part of his dreams. But the thing I thought about most, when I was in my room, lying on the bed, was that there was something real about the dream that I didn't know how to explain but that I could feel. When I closed my eyes and thought about people tying the man up, and some of them drinking soda, I felt weak, too, as if I didn't have any strength. I tried to move my legs, and I could. I was so glad I could.

I asked Loren who he thought he was to call a meeting.

"I just called it," he said. "Somebody has to do something about Mr. Moses."

"My mother thinks that the most important thing is that he gets enough to eat." Sessi was sitting cross-legged against one of the chimneys. It was hot, and the smell of the tar roof was stronger than it usually was.

Loren started talking about how the most important thing was that Mr. Moses had a place to live. He said that if he was hungry it would be bad, but it would be worse if he didn't have any place to go. Kimi said if Mr. Moses was sick, he needed medicine.

"My mom said he could have Alzheimer's disease," Loren said.

"He doesn't forget," I said, "he remembers. That's what makes him so tired all the time. He told me another one of his dreams yesterday."

"In Africa we look to the elders for wisdom," Sessi said. "When an elder speaks, we listen, and even if we don't agree, we show them respect."

"What was this dream about?" Loren asked.

"It was about a man who was arrested for breaking into somebody's house," I said.

"Why did he do that?" Sessi asked. "Was he poor?"

"Mr. Moses said he was innocent," I said. "But he was poor and black, and the jury found him guilty. Then some men took him from the jail and hung him. They lynched him and made his friends and family watch while they did it."

"What they did to black people in this country is terrible." Sessi turned away. "It's a terrible part of your history."

"It's the watching Mr. Moses dreams about. Watching something terrible like that and not being able to do anything about it. The people got weak and couldn't move."

"Some people in my family, the ones who haven't lived a long time in the city, think that you can take a person's strength from them if you get some of their hair and boil it," Sessi said. "We were taught not to believe that, but a lot of people talk about it."

"Mr. Moses don't fool around!" Loren said. "He's got

some dreams that will blow your mind. He dreams stuff on slavery, and on Africa, and all kinds of stuff you read in books."

"Could he be making them up?" Kimi leaned forward.

"I don't think so," I said. "When he tells his dreams, they don't sound like something made up. They seem to come from someplace deep inside of him."

"My grandmother said she once knew a woman who died of grief two days after her husband," Sessi said.

"Was she old?" Loren asked.

"The woman who died?"

"Your grandmother," Loren said.

"She is really old." Sessi wiped at the tip of her nose with her finger. "I know she was seventy-two last year, because we received a card from her family."

"Seventy-two isn't old," Loren said. "Mr. Moses said he's about three hundred years old."

"Nobody is that old," Sessi said.

"Did the woman get weak before she died?" I asked.

"My grandmother didn't say," Sessi said. "And I don't want to talk about it anymore. You know, it's bad to talk about the dead."

"That sounds like more African stuff." Loren gave me a look. He seemed uncomfortable. "You want to come to my house and watch television?"

"Do you have people in Africa who keep dreams?" I asked Sessi. "Mr. Moses said that it's his responsibility to remember all these dreams."

"How is it his responsibility?" Sessi asked. "Nobody should have to dream if they don't want to. If I had to dream when I didn't want to, I wouldn't want to go to sleep."

"He calls them dreams, but when I think about them, the way he tells them, they're like a way of seeing into people, a way of knowing what their visions are all about," I answered.

"I don't want to dream anything bad." Kimi was getting nervous. "When I go to bed, I don't want to dream at all. All I want to do is sleep."

"Some people believe in magic." Sessi leaned forward. "In Africa there are people who say they can see the future in their dreams."

"I've never heard of that." Loren was shaking his head.

"It's not something you put into the papers, silly," Sessi said. "Especially in the United States, because nobody believes anything in this country."

"We could take a collection for him," Kimi said.

"My father says that people have to make their own way in the world, and you shouldn't help everybody just because they look sad," Loren said. "He doesn't like people begging."

"He gets mad at them?" Kimi asked.

"He doesn't go off like David's father," Loren said.

As soon as the words came out of his mouth, Loren

knew they were wrong. They made me feel terrible. The tears came to my eyes and they were burning, and I wanted to hit Loren for saying what he did. Sessi looked at me and saw how I felt and tried to put her arm around me. I pushed her away and then I got up and started downstairs.

Loren is my best friend and I like him so much, and he knows everything about me and I know everything about him, but sometimes there are things we don't talk about. One of those things is Reuben.

I didn't like Loren talking about Reuben, but by the time I got downstairs, I wasn't upset about it. Just thinking about what Reuben might do, and never knowing at any moment just how he would act, kept me a little nervous. I had some milk and a banana and then checked my e-mail and found a message from Loren. It said, "I'm sorry." There was a sad-face symbol next to it.

Mom had folded my pajamas and put them on the end of the bed. I put them on and lay across the bed. I was thinking about what Sessi had said, that no one should have to dream if they didn't want to, including Mr. Moses.

The dreams were important to Mr. Moses, but they were things he had seen and done, or at least things that he knew about. They were his dreams. He said he was tired of having them, that he had been a dream bearer for hundreds of years and wanted to pass them on. But if they were his dreams, how could he pass them on? I knew he was telling them to me for a reason. I didn't want to have bad dreams, or to get stuck with something that I would dream over and over. But the more dreams he told me, the more I could feel them—not explain them or even talk about them the way Mr. Moses did, but feel them. And even though they were new, I felt as if maybe I had heard them before, or knew something about them.

There were things I knew. I knew that Loren felt bad about dissing Reuben. He didn't have to send the sad face in his message. I knew that Ty was struggling with how he was living. I knew that Mom was trying to be strong enough for all of us.

Reuben. He protected his dreams, kept them hidden inside himself, but I knew they were there. Maybe Reuben's dreams were waiting for someone to feel them, to understand them.

If something bad happened to Loren, I might dream about that, but not about some man I didn't know who had died a long time ago.

Mom came home and looked in my room.

"David, are you asleep?" she asked softly.

"Yes, I am," I said.

"Stinker! How did your day go?"

"Okay. Maybe even pretty good."

She came to the bed and kissed me on the forehead. "Good night, and thanks for being wonderful," she said.

Her saying that made me feel good.

I was almost asleep when I thought of something else. If I could dream what Reuben dreamed, what he was dreaming when he made noises in his sleep and swung his arms around, maybe I would know him better.

Ty started getting into a gangster strut. On 145th Street they call people like Ty—straight dudes who want to act as if they're really rough—WGs. I didn't mind him being a wanna-be gangster, but it bugged me that he laid it on Mom.

"I don't want Mom to have to deal with it and I don't want to deal with it," I said.

"Who died and made you Punk of the Year?" Ty was looking at me in the mirror. "You ain't running my show."

"Are you running it?" I asked him. "Are you running your show? You look like you're doing more slipping and sliding than running anything."

"You still living in that fantasy land of yours? What

do you call it? I Hope Everything Comes Out All Rightville?"

"You give up hope for yourself and you messing with Mom and—everything," I said.

"What were you going to say? Mom and Reuben? He's probably going to nut out and then we'll be calling him Little Red Riding Hood or something," Ty said. "Maybe if he dies, you'll get a chance to go to college on his insurance money."

"He's okay," I said.

"Okay? How's he going to be okay when you're the man of the house?" Ty asked. "Mom got to take care of his sorry butt more than she got to take care of you."

Mom came into the room in a huff. I knew she had heard what Ty was saying.

"There was a time, young man, when you couldn't take care of yourself," Mom said. "You were crawling around on the floor and peeing in your diapers, and your father took enough care of you so that you weren't hungry and you weren't cold. And don't forget you're living in his house—he's not living in yours!" she said. "I hope that's clear to you."

"Yeah, it's clear," Ty said, picking up the sports section of the paper.

The phone rang and Mom answered it. She nodded a few times and looked at me and Ty, then told whoever it was to wait a minute and put her hand over the mouthpiece. "It's Sessi's mother," she said. "She just got her permanent status and wants us to come over for tea. I would like both of you to come with me."

"Yeah, sure." Ty closed his paper.

We went over the roof to Sessi's house, and Mom saw the little building that Sessi had built. Ty said it looked like a doghouse. Even the WG knew how weak that comment was.

Mrs. Mutu had made hot tea and iced tea and had a huge plate of cookies. Loren and his mom were there, and naturally she was going on about how wonderful it was that such lovely people were going to become Americans.

Loren was looking at me but I wouldn't look at him. I wasn't mad at him, but I wanted him to know I wasn't that glad about what he had said either.

"If Sessi married an American, she would automatically be an American, right?" I asked.

"Are you proposing marriage to my daughter, young man?" Mr. Mutu was short and wore dark horn-rimmed glasses.

"No," I said. "I just asked."

"That used to be the law," Mr. Mutu said. "It's been changed quite a bit since then."

They started talking about what America meant to everybody, and I thought about what Reuben had said— that it was easier for somebody from another country to become an American than it was for him. I wanted to say something about that, but I didn't. I didn't because I knew they wouldn't understand me. And if I mentioned Reuben, I knew, they wouldn't understand him, either. I said I had to go. Loren asked his mother if he could go with me. She said yes without even asking me if I wanted him to go with me.

Ty went downstairs, and me and Loren went up to the roof.

"I'm sorry about what I said about your father," he said. "He doesn't get that mad."

"Yes he does," I said.

"Then why did you get mad?"

"Just because something is true doesn't mean you have to say it," I said.

"You want to get into Sessi's house?" Loren asked.

"No."

"What do you think we should do about Mr. Moses if he's still sick?"

"You just want to talk," I said. "That's what you always do. You say something that makes somebody feel bad, and then you want to bug out by talking about some off-the-wall thing."

"First he said that first guy got hung," Loren went on, "then he said the next guy got weak. Maybe if you can't take care of your friends, you get weak."

The door opened and Reuben came out onto the roof. He looked around and at us and then came over. "Where's your mom?" he asked me.

"Down at Sessi's house," I said. "Sessi is a permanent

resident now, and they're having tea and cookies. Ty was there, too. He went downstairs."

"Yeah, I saw him." Reuben leaned against the little wall that separated the roofs. "You know, when I was a kid, my family used to have picnics on the roof."

"Really!" Loren said, like he was really surprised or something.

"We'd bring a couple of folding card tables up here," Reuben said. "We'd put the food on one of them and play cards on the other one. On holidays you could see people having picnics all over the neighborhood, up on the roofs. Then sometimes my best friend and I would come up on the roof and make model planes. We'd make them out of balsa wood, paint them up and everything. Or maybe we would just sit up on the roof and catch the breeze and talk like you guys are doing."

"We're talking about Mr. Moses' dreams," Loren said.

I wished he hadn't said it.

Reuben looked away across the street. For a moment I thought he might be seeing a picnic going on, and I turned and looked, but I didn't see any.

"I'm thinking of going downstairs for supper," Loren said.

That made me smile, because I knew that Loren was sorry he had said anything about Mr. Moses' dreams in front of Reuben. He said he would e-mail me later.

"You gave your mother your password?" I asked.

"No!"

"She's got it," I said. "She answered the e-mail I sent you."

"She got it?" Loren got on his mad look and then went downstairs.

"You going downstairs?" I asked Reuben.

"What is he, some kind of father figure to you?" Reuben asked. "I'm talking about the old man."

"No, he's just interesting," I said.

"What were you and Loren talking about?"

"Just about this and that," I said. "Nothing special."

"You guys talking man talk?"

"I don't know," I said. "I guess."

"You feel like a man?"

"I don't know how a man is supposed to feel," I said.

"How a man is supposed to feel?" He repeated what I had said. "Well, you got a space around you, right?"

"Yeah?"

"It could be a small space, just where you standing, or a big space, like your house or the block you live on. If you're a man, you control your space. You don't have any control, you got to wonder if you're a man. You control your space?"

I thought about it for a while, and I didn't think I really controlled any space and said so. Reuben told me not to worry about it, he would control my space until I could handle it for myself.

※◈※

HEN$ON CRI$I$

The Matthew Henson Community Project has reached crunch time. Deputy Mayor Alex Hund announced today that the appellate court has sent the case back to the state supreme court to deal with the claim of Robert Kerlin, the owner of the building, as to his right to sell or develop the building as he chooses or, minimally, to determine the fair market value of the property. A member of the Henson Project committee suggested that if Kerlin set the price, it would be without a doubt beyond the finances of the committee unless the City of New York assumed a great deal of the financial burden.

"Of course, that would stop it from being a community project," said the committee member, who asked not to be identified.

As soon as the paper came out, the phone started ringing. Mom kept telling people she wasn't involved anymore, but I could tell she was emotionally still in it.

I told her about Mr. Moses needing someone to take care of him and that the Henson Project would have been perfect for him. She told me not to make too much of it in front of Reuben.

Reuben was working in Mr. Kerlin's building every day and sometimes at night, too. That was all he seemed to think about. Even when Mom told him that Ty was thinking about not going back to school, he didn't say anything about it. I thought about telling him that I was thinking about dropping out too, just to see what he would say. I knew I wasn't going to drop out and didn't have the nerve to make a joke with Reuben.

A disaster happened. I had been thinking a lot about controlling my space. When I told Loren what Reuben had said about that, he said he always controlled his space. I told him he couldn't control his nose, let alone his space. He said he could control me and jumped toward me just as I got my hands up. He got a little punch on the nose and it started bleeding immediately. We were on the stoop, and I took him across the street to the church and a woman put some ice in a towel and put it on his nose. Then I had to take him back across the street to the stoop, with him walking with his head way back and the ice cubes on his nose. The disaster came when we got back to the stoop and his mother, who was just coming in from work, saw him with his head back and blood on the towel.

She started screaming and stuff and asking what happened. Loren said that I hit him when he wasn't looking, and Mrs. Hart really started screaming at me and saying that she had to move away from this terrible neighborhood. She tried to pick Loren up to carry him upstairs, but he's too big and so he had to walk.

"Hoodlum!" That's what she yelled at me over her shoulder.

And old stupid Loren was just going to let her make a big fuss over him because he likes when she does that.

Then Sessi came downstairs and asked me why I had punched Loren in the nose. I started to explain and she said she didn't want to hear my explanation.

"I might have to go back to Kenya to get away from so much of violence," she said, with a big smile on her face.

Loren can make me feel worse than anybody in the whole world. I went upstairs and told Mom what had happened, and about Loren's mother calling me a hoodlum. Mom told me I should apologize to Loren even if it was an accident.

"Friends learn to be kind to each other," she said.

I decided to e-mail Loren on his superhero line. Soon as I got online, I saw that I had a message from him. It said that we should take Mr. Moses up to the roof to see Sessi's house, that if he didn't have anyplace else to go, he could live there. That was a good idea and I was mad that Loren had it instead of me. I e-mailed him that I would think about it.

I called Sessi and she said that Loren had already called her and told her about the idea.

"He's very bright," she said.

He was also very fast.

Loren got a cell phone. Mrs. Hart bought it for him after I hit him in the nose.

"I told her I was thinking of knocking you out, and she said that I had to be careful so I wouldn't get a juvenile record," Loren said.

"You couldn't knock me out if you had a baseball bat," I said. We were on the park bench because I had got tired of beating Loren one-on-one. We had also played some two-on-two with two guys from 143rd Street, and they were better than we were but we still beat them because they tried to get too fancy. Loren had brought some bread crumbs for the birds, but he also had a piece of chocolate in his pocket and most of the crumbs stuck to that.

"Here he comes!" Loren said.

It was Mr. Moses. He was walking slow, more like he was doing it on purpose than being tired or anything. He came toward us and he smiled a little when he got right near us.

"You boys are always together," Mr. Moses said. "I like to see that in young men. Friends are more important than gold and silver."

"I'm his bodyguard," Loren said.

"Well, that's good, too," Mr. Moses said.

"You want to go see a real African house?" Loren asked. "We got one right up on the roof. We'll take you to see it if you want."

Mr. Moses looked at Loren and then he looked at me.

"It's not that much," I said. "Our friend Sessi Mutu made it. She's African. That's her name, Sessi Mutu."

"She built this house up on our roof out of grass and sticks and string," Loren said. "It's not big or anything, but it looks like a real African house, or at least probably does. Sessi was born in Africa."

"Well, if you want me to go see it, I will," Mr. Moses said.

Soon as Loren started talking, I changed my mind about taking Mr. Moses up all those stairs. Sessi's house was okay for us, but it wasn't all that much for a grown-up.

"Can I ask you something about your dreams?" I asked him.

"Yes, yes." He nodded slowly. Then he turned and sat down. Loren moved over and gave him some room.

"When that guy made you the dream bearer, did he give you the dreams, too?"

"I thought he did," Mr. Moses said. "For a long time I thought he was giving me the heavy dreams he had. Then one day I saw that I had forgotten his dreams and had my own."

"You ever have any funny dreams?" Loren asked.

"One dream makes me smile sometimes," Mr. Moses said. "When it don't make me sad. And sometimes it makes me sad, when it don't make me smile."

"What's the dream?" Loren took his chocolate bar out, brushed off a few crumbs, and bit off the end of it.

"I once heard about a blind man who could beat anybody in the county playing checkers," Mr. Moses said. "He was born blind but he learned all the moves of checkers and got to be an expert. People came from far away as Tupelo to play against him. But the first thing he'd do was to ask whoever he was set to play what color they was. He said he had to play black people different from white people. When I dream about him, I picture him peering through his darkness looking for something he ain't never seen. And sometimes I think I see it and it makes me laugh, and sometimes I think I see it and it fills my cup with tears."

"If he's blind, he can't see anything," Loren said.

"We see," Mr. Moses said. "Eyes or not, we see. And

sometimes what we see when we're not using our eyes is the only thing what's real. Now you boys going to show me that house on the roof?"

I told Mr. Moses that if he didn't want to go up the stairs it was okay.

He said he would go and we started to the house. He was walking so slow, I figured he wasn't going to make it. I wanted to say I changed my mind and he shouldn't come, but the more I didn't say it and the more he walked, the worse I felt about not saying it when I first thought about it. We got to my stoop and Loren went ahead and I followed.

When Loren went up the stairs he kind of hopped from one side of the stairs to the other. Mr. Moses went after Loren, and he was pulling himself up by the banister and leaning on it when he made the turn. I thought we would never get to the roof. By the time we got to the top floor, I could hear Mr. Moses' breathing. When he breathed, he made two little sucking noises and then one noise that sounded like a sigh. I knew me and Loren shouldn't have had him come up so many stairs, and I was feeling ashamed.

It had rained earlier and it was a cloudy day, but when we got to the roof, the sun had come out and the sky had brightened. I looked over at Sessi's little house and saw that the rain had washed it down and it looked better than I had ever seen it looking.

"Whoa! Look at that!" Mr. Moses said. "Now that's a

beautiful house. It's beautiful to behold."

"You ever seen anything like that before?" Loren asked.

"I might have," Mr. Moses said. "Things ain't as clear to me as they used to be. But when I stand here and look at this house, I think I've seen it before. Maybe it was a hundred years ago, or maybe longer than that. You know how memory hides behind doors and jumps out at you or slips by in the dark."

"You look inside if you want," Loren said, like Sessi's house belonged to him.

Mr. Moses moved aside the door that Sessi had made and looked inside. Then he started to walk around the house. When he did that, I looked inside the house too. You couldn't see much in there except where the light came down through a hole she had put in the roof. The light coming down through the grass made a round pattern on the floor, which was really the roof. I started thinking that we should get a rug or some mats and make a regular floor.

Then Mr. Moses started coughing. It wasn't a big cough, but he kept on doing it. I looked at Loren and he looked back at me, like we do sometimes when we don't know what else to do.

When Mr. Moses sat down on the roof, leaning against the little wall that separated one roof from the next, I got scared. He was coughing and I could see he couldn't control it. It was a little after two o'clock and

Loren's parents were working. I thought that Reuben was downstairs, but I didn't want to tell him what had happened.

Mr. Moses kept coughing and Loren got to looking real sad. I looked him right in the face and he was making words with his mouth like I was supposed to read his lips or something, but I couldn't read them at all. I knew what I was thinking, that Mr. Moses might get sick and die.

"I'm going downstairs for a minute." I knelt down in front of Mr. Moses and spoke right at his face. He looked terrible. "You want some water or something?"

He didn't say anything, but he was tipping over to one side.

"Stay with him!" I told Loren.

Loren looked scared but I didn't care. I ran down the stairs two at a time with a jump at the end of each section and went to my house. I was hoping that Reuben would be up but he wasn't.

I shook Reuben's shoulder, and he jumped up and knocked my hands away.

"What you want?! What you want?!" he yelled, and was looking around.

"We took Mr. Moses up on the roof and I think he's sick up there," I said.

"He touch you?" Reuben's eyes were big and mad looking.

"No, I just think he's dying," I said.

"Let him die!"

"No!" I backed away and bumped into the closet. "We can't let somebody die."

"How he get up on the roof?"

"Me and Loren took him to show him Sessi's house," I said. "You saw Sessi's house."

"He wanted to go up there?" His voice wasn't so mad anymore.

"We asked him to go," I said. "Can you help him? We can bring him some water."

Mom had made some iced tea that was in a jar in the refrigerator, and Reuben got that and told me to wet a towel with cold water, and I did that while he put some ice cubes in a bowl. I didn't know why he got the ice cubes but I was glad he was doing it.

We went up to the roof. Loren was standing at the side of Sessi's house with his eyes closed.

"Is he dead?" I asked.

Mr. Moses wasn't dead, but he was really sick. Reuben put his fingers on his neck and then gave him some iced tea. He put the towel on his neck and told me to go downstairs and call 911.

"I got a cell phone!" Loren said.

Loren called 911 and told them we had a really sick old man on the roof. We waited for fifteen minutes before we heard an ambulance siren in the street below. I waved to them from the edge of the roof and motioned for them to come up. It seemed a long time, but finally two firemen and some emergency medical technicians showed up.

They put Mr. Moses on a stretcher and carried him down the stairs.

Ambulances and police cars are always running up and down 145th Street, so them taking away Mr. Moses was no big deal. Loren's mom came home, and she ran up to him and started hugging him and asking him if he was all right. He pushed away from her, but I know he liked it.

"Thanks," I said to Reuben.

"No big thing," he said.

He meant that. I had never seen him do anything for anybody before, but he could just fit it in so easy when he wanted. For me it was exciting, and scary. To Reuben it was no big thing. I think even Loren was surprised.

When they took Mr. Moses to the hospital, I felt terrible. It was the same feeling I had when Reuben hit Ty and knocked him down. My stomach started cramping and my mouth was really dry. What I thought was that he was going to die. Mr. Moses wasn't really a friend of mine, and I didn't know that much about him, but I was comfortable with him, the way I'm comfortable with Mom and Loren and, once in a while, Ty. Reuben got real quiet. Even when I asked him if he thought Mr. Moses was going to be all right, he didn't answer.

When I got home, I got a call from Loren. He was calling me on his cell phone. He said that maybe we shouldn't have asked Mr. Moses to come up to the roof.

"They took him to Harlem Hospital," he said. "You

want to go down there tomorrow?"

"Yeah, okay," I said. "I can go if you want to. Your mother is going to let you go with me?"

"I don't need her permission," Loren said.

"Yes you do," I said. "Because if she says no and you go, and she tells your father, he's going to tear your butt up."

"You think I might have to knock him out?"

"Yeah. Right," I said. "Anyway, we can go in the morning. They won't let us go upstairs to see him, but we can ask about him."

"We can buy a card and leave it for him."

That was another good idea, and I was mad again because I didn't think of it. "Yeah, okay."

When Mom got home, she brought ground meat and asked me if I wanted to help make supper. Reuben had already gone to work, so I didn't mind helping Mom. I chopped up a big onion and cooked it in butter and curry sauce. Then I mixed it in the hamburger like Mom taught me while she made potato salad.

"Is the old man homeless?" Mom asked.

"He says that nobody is homeless," I said. "There are just some people away from their homes. But I guess he's away from his. I don't know if he has a regular place to live."

"Does he drink?"

I looked over at Mom. She was cutting up tomatoes to go on the salad. She chopped fast, with both hands on the knife. "I don't know if he ever drinks, but I never smell liquor on him."

"Do you get close to him?"

"Close enough to hear him," I said. "But he doesn't bother me and Loren or touch us. I know what that means."

"I didn't say he touched you." Mom put the knife down. "I was just wondering how you came to be friends."

"We're not really friends, but he's interesting," I said. "He knows things that I want to know about."

"Sometimes knowing a lot isn't that useful," Mom said.

She went on talking about a girl she had gone to school with who had been very smart but got messed up because she fell in love with the wrong boy and they got into trouble together. It surprised me for her to say that. It surprised me because we were using the same words, how a person knew something, but we were meaning different things.

We finished making the hamburgers, and Mom asked me if I wanted to eat right away or wait to see if Ty and Reuben would be home. I said I would wait and we put the food in the refrigerator.

In my room I imagined the smart girl Mom had mentioned. Being smart like that wasn't what I had meant, but I couldn't come up with the right words. I thought Mr. Moses knew things, things that were so deep inside you that maybe you didn't know them yourself, but he did. He knew about people and what was going on inside of them. I wondered: If I knew all that stuff, if I had been learning more and more about it and got old and stored it up, what would I do with it? Would it be something wonderful, or would it be heavy in my head all the time and wearing me down?

Loren called.

"I got grounded," he said. "For calling Africa."

"Africa?"

"I got the number of Sessi's aunt," Loren said. "So I called her to see if the cell phone could call that far. I told my mom, and she grounded me and the phone."

"You tell her you saved Mr. Moses' life?" I asked.

"No!" I could hear Loren running to tell his mom that he had saved Mr. Moses' life with his cell phone.

We went to Harlem Hospital, on 135th Street and Malcolm X Boulevard, on Monday, Tuesday, and Wednesday. Each time the woman downstairs said he was okay. On Thursday, though, she said he had been discharged.

That was good, because I wanted to see him again. I wanted him to see Loren again so I could tell him it was Loren who called for the ambulance. I would tell him we could have gone downstairs and called from my house, but the way it happened was that Loren, my friend, made the phone call, and I was proud of that.

We went to the park on Friday and on Saturday, but Mr. Moses wasn't there. We went down to Harlem Hospital Saturday afternoon after the Mets game and I asked if I could get his address, and the lady said a grown-up would have to make that request.

"And you're a long way from being grown, young man," she said.

"That's true," Loren said, "but I'm his father."

I asked Ty to call and he said no. I said he was a turkey, except I didn't say it out loud.

Monday morning. I could smell breakfast cooking and went out and saw that Mom and Ty were in the kitchen.

"You want something to eat?" Mom asked.

Mom looked calm, and so did Ty. Mom had on her Sunday dress, and I thought maybe they were going downtown. I sat down next to Ty, and Mom took two eggs out of the carton, cracked them one at a time into a bowl, and started scrambling them. I'm the only one in the house who likes scrambled eggs, so I knew they were for me.

"Where you going?"

"To take care of some business," Mom said. She put on a smile and looked over to where Ty was sitting.

We all ate, and then Mom kissed me on the forehead, which I hate when she does, and she and Ty left. She asked me to stay home until they got back.

I figured it had something to do with Ty and it didn't seem like Mom was upset, so I figured it was okay. There wasn't much on television except some people selling machines to make your stomach smaller and some other people selling barbecue grills, and some cartoons. I started watching the cartoons.

I must have fallen asleep—I was tired a lot recently—and woke up when I heard Mom and Ty talking outside of my room. They had just come in, and Mom was saying to Ty that maybe he should be more careful in choosing his friends.

"They're just a bunch of punks!" Ty said.

"Honey, let it go," Mom said. "It's settled."

"It's not going to happen again," Ty said. "You can bank on that."

"Four hundred dollars is a lot of money," Mom said. "And it's money we don't have."

I went out into the kitchen. Ty had on his wanna-be face, and Mom was getting uptight.

"Hi," I said.

"Yeah," Ty answered gruffly.

"Ty, you want to go down to Thirty-fourth Street with me? I need some towels and—"

"No," Ty said.

"What happened?" I asked.

"Your brother made some foolish bets," Mom said. "And he couldn't cover them."

"Bets on what?" I asked, looking dead at my brother.

"Baseball games, basketball games, whatever," Ty said. "I blew it, and Mom got the money together and paid it off. I'll pay it back."

It wasn't true. None of what Ty said was true. Mom started cleaning the stove, putting spray cleaner on the porcelain sides and talking about how Ty had to choose his friends more carefully. Ty glared at me, and I glared right back. Mom needed to believe him. I didn't.

"Even if you're doing the right thing, you can be hurt by people who aren't." She took the plates off the table and put them into the hot, soapy dishwater.

"There are vipers out there, man. You just don't know who they are," Ty said.

"That's true, son," Mom replied.

But everything they were saying was wrong. They were making it up, but at the same time they weren't making it up. They were hoping that it was real.

Ty said he was going to go to the library. He kissed Mom and thanked her for helping him out. He asked me if I wanted to go with him.

"No."

When he had gone, Mom sat down. She still had the dishrag in her hands.

"Sometimes when you're dealing with family," she said, "you have to understand that family is more important than anything else you have. I sure hope you don't ever get into any trouble, but if you do, all of us will be there for you, the same as we were there for Ty."

"How do you know what he's saying is true?" I asked. "You want it to be true and you make it easy for him to say it, but how do you know it's true?"

"I know because I have faith in your brother!" Mom said. "The same as I have faith in you, David. Don't you think I have faith in you?"

"Yes, I do."

I knew that Mom wanted things to be different, and maybe Ty wanted things to be different, too. I thought they hadn't talked it over or anything, they had come to an agreement about what they wanted to say was the truth.

Maybe it was okay for Ty, but I knew it was just going to hurt Mom more. I didn't think Ty was gambling. I thought he was messing with drugs.

Mom asked me to go shopping with her. We went down to 125th Street and walked across town, stopping in a few stores. I asked her what we were going to buy.

"I'm looking for some nice material to make drapes for the living room," she said.

"The sewing machine is fixed?"

"No, but if I buy the material, maybe that will inspire me to get it fixed," she said. "When I was a girl living with my parents on St. Nicholas Avenue, my mother would make something new every Christmas. Sometimes it would be new curtains, sometimes she'd make a tablecloth. It was her way of announcing that the season had arrived."

We stopped in the Studio Museum store and looked

around at the books, and Mom bought some note cards. When we came out, the sun was hot and nice against my skin.

"I don't know if Tyrone is still in trouble or not," Mom said.

"I thought you paid off the money he owed."

"When people get into debt like that—when they owe money out and people threaten them about it—it's usually more serious than just dollars changing hands."

"So what do you think the problem is?" I asked. I remembered how hard she had been trying to believe Ty.

"I don't know," Mom said. "I hope I'm just an overly worried mother. What do you think?"

"Sometimes we want things to be all right," I said.

"Good," she said, as if she hadn't heard what I had said. "But you keep your eyes open anyway. All right?"

"Sure."

We walked all the way across 125th Street and looked in about ten stores without buying anything else. It was as if we were on a minivacation, and I didn't say anything more about Ty.

We took the A train back up to 145th Street and walked down the hill to the house. On the way upstairs Mom said that Loren's mom had called her just to talk. She didn't say anything about me hitting Loren in the nose.

"I think she just wanted to chat," Mom said.

"That's just the way Loren is," I said. "When something

happens and he wants to get past it, he just talks about something else. He's probably got a gene from his mother or something."

Mom started saying something about how people learn things from their families as she opened the door. Soon as she got it open, she stopped talking and kind of gasped.

When I looked past her, I saw that the kitchen was all messed up. There were broken dishes on the table and on the floor, and the wall calendar was torn with part of it still hanging from the nail.

"Reuben?" Mom called softly.

"You want me to get the police?"

"Wait," she said. "Reuben?" she called louder.

The door to Mom's bedroom was closed, but we could hear noises coming from it. It sounded like the radio. I took a step toward the door and Mom stopped me. Then she took my hand. When we pushed the door open, we could hear the radio, and the crying. Reuben was lying on the bed. He was all curled up in a tight knot, and his hands were over his face. The blanket was lying across his legs.

Mom glanced around the room and then moved the blanket away to look under it. Then she pulled it over his shoulders.

"Reuben, is everything— Can I do anything?"

He didn't answer, just kept crying. It was like he wasn't crying out of himself but was crying into himself. That's how soft it was. His body was shaking, too, and I began to shake a little bit and I could feel I was going to cry.

I followed Mom back out to the kitchen, and she sat down at the table and took two really deep breaths. There was cold water in the refrigerator, and I poured some into a glass and gave it to her.

"What do you think is wrong?"

"I don't know," she said. Her eyes were already teary. "Just give me a minute to figure out what to do."

We sat in the kitchen for a while. I thought about picking up all the broken glass, but I thought I would wait to see what Mom was going to do.

"Do you think we should bring his medicine to him?" I asked.

Mom shook her head. "I don't know," she said.

I wanted to do something, but I didn't know what. Reuben had been bad before, but this time it looked worse than ever. I had thought, up on the roof with Mr. Moses, that I was closer to Reuben. Or that he was closer to me and things might be going in the right direction. Maybe I had made that up, the way that Mom had made up solving Ty's problems.

The clock on the wall ticked loudly, slowly. Outside somebody was passing by with a radio, and I could hear the music get louder and then softer as they passed.

When the knock on the door came, I jumped. Mom looked at me and then sat up straight in her chair like she was getting ready to face whoever was knocking. I thought it might be the police, that somebody had heard Reuben breaking up stuff and called them.

I opened the door. A young white woman with dark hair stood in the hallway.

"Is this the Curry household?" she asked.

"Honey, whatever you have, we don't want any today," Mom said over my shoulder.

"I'm an intern from the *Amsterdam News*." The white girl spoke quickly. "And I just wanted to get your reaction to the settlement of the Matthew Henson Community Project."

For three days Reuben didn't get out of bed except to go to the bathroom. For three days Mom brought his food in to him and put it on the table next to the bed, but he didn't eat it. When she said we had to watch him, I asked her why but I already knew the answer. She was afraid he was going to hurt himself. I was afraid too.

One morning I went into the bathroom and there were drops of blood on the sink. My heart started beating like crazy, and for a while I couldn't catch my breath. But then I remembered I had seen blood drops on the sink before. I didn't want to tell Mom. Not just yet, not until we saw what was going to happen with Reuben.

The bathroom door locked, and I figured that's why Ty took his drugs in there. I wondered if he looked at himself in the mirror when he used the needle. I wondered if your own image could frighten you. Ty was asleep and snoring loudly when I returned to bed after seeing the blood. Lying in the darkness, I realized I felt better knowing that it was Ty hurting himself than Reuben. I had seen junkies on the street before, had even brushed by them in the hallway. It was something bad I knew about. Reuben was still far away from anything I could relate to.

The story about the Henson Project was in both of the papers I read. There was the picture of Mr. Kerlin, a big cigar sticking out of his mouth, saying how he had decided to make a major contribution to the community.

"What he's done," Mom said, "is make a lot of money by selling his building to the city. The Henson Project is going to lease it from the city instead of buying it."

"And what's going to happen to Reuben?" I asked.

Her mouth tightened up and she shook her head. "He dumped your father the same way he dumped the building," she said after a while.

"That just stinks," I said.

"It's his right to do what he wants with his building," Mom said. "He owned the building and he had the right to sell it. If I owned the building and could have made a lot of money on it, I don't know if I would have done anything different."

"I think you would have," I said.

Mom watched Reuben at night. She got him to drink

water and juice, but he still didn't eat any regular food. He just kept lying in the bed, mostly with the lights out.

We took turns watching Reuben. Mom wanted one of us to be in the house all the time to look in on him. Ty said he didn't want to watch Reuben because he was a cripple. He didn't say it in front of Mom, but he spit the words out to me when we were in our room.

"I know you're using," I said. "I saw the blood from the needle on the sink."

"You don't know nothing, jerk!" he sneered.

"Tell me about how I'm a jerk, Ty," I said to him. "Tell me how I'm a punk and Reuben's a cripple and all the dudes on the street are punks."

"Maybe if I kicked your butt you'd understand why you're a jerk," he answered, half standing.

"Yeah, maybe." I stood and faced him.

He came over and pulled his fist back as if he was going to punch me, forced out a phony laugh, and grabbed his jacket. I knew he was headed for the streets.

Loren said he would come over and help watch Reuben when it was my turn. "We can watch him together and play chess."

"He'll be okay," I said. "I just got to watch him a little bit when Mom goes out shopping or down to the Social Security office."

I didn't want Loren to see Reuben lying on the bed.

Loren was my best friend in the world, but it still made me feel bad for him to see how Reuben looked. When he was awake he would be very still, his eyes almost shut but not quite. If I came into the room, I wouldn't know if he saw me or not. But when he was asleep it was worse. He would be twitching and moving his arms around as if something was coming at him. Sometimes he would make whimpering noises, like a child. I didn't want Loren to see any of this, and I didn't want him to talk about it either.

I didn't think things could get worse, but they did. On Thursday night I woke up and heard Mom yelling. It was three minutes past four o'clock.

"Reuben, *please!*" Mom was yelling.

I got my pants on as fast as I could and ran into the kitchen. Mom was in her bathrobe, and Reuben had his clothes on and was tying up his shoes.

"Where can you go this time of night?" Mom asked. "Where can you go? *Please!*"

I ran back to my room and turned on the light. I shook Ty but I couldn't get him up. He smelled bad, like he might have been drinking. My old sneakers were in front of the closet, and I got them on just as I heard the front door close.

"Don't go after him," Mom said, as she passed me. "I'll get dressed and we'll get a cab."

"You know where he's going?"

"No," I heard her call.

There was no way we would find him if we waited for Mom to get dressed. I grabbed a shirt and went out the door and down the stairs.

When I got down to the stoop, I didn't see him. It was rainy and cold and dark, and the streets were almost empty.

"Hey! Boy!"

Across the street there was a couple standing near the street lamp. The man was pointing toward the corner near the grocery store.

I looked and didn't see anything, but I ran across the street anyway. My sneakers weren't tied but they didn't fall off. When I got to the corner, I looked down the street and saw Reuben walking and moving his hands like he was talking to somebody. I walked faster but stayed a little way behind him. When I got kind of close, I stopped and tied my sneakers.

I thought about calling to him and asking him not to go, but I didn't know what to say. Mom had already asked him not to go. So we walked through the rain a while, him in front about fifteen steps ahead of me. Sometimes I could hear him talking, but I didn't know what he was saying except I could hear the word "man."

We were headed downtown and he was walking fast, but I didn't mind. I could keep up with him. When we reached the corner of 135th Street, near the hospital, he looked back and saw me. He just stood on the corner for a minute looking at me. I didn't know what to do, so I lifted my chin, the way Loren does sometimes when he wants people to think he's not afraid.

Reuben turned away again and continued walking. The rain came down harder. The rain was warm but I was getting soaked and cold. We walked all the way down to 125th Street, and then he started across town, heading west. I didn't think he knew where he was going, but I was glad it was a long way. The walking calmed me down a little even though I was still scared.

Reuben stopped when we reached St. Joseph's Church and turned toward me.

"What you want?" he asked. His voice came out like a growl.

I didn't say anything. I just stood and looked back at him. I couldn't get my chin up again but I kept looking at him.

As he went farther, he staggered a little. I knew he hadn't been drinking and thought he might be sick. We went past the George Bruce Library and the Cotton

Club, to where the streets are made of cobblestones, and a car almost hit him. The guy in the car yelled out the window, and Reuben went back and kicked the fender.

My heart was beating fast when the car backed up. I thought it was going to run into Reuben, but it just circled around him with the driver yelling and cursing as he went by.

Reuben kept walking, and I saw we were headed toward the river.

There wasn't anything pretty about the Hudson River off 125th Street. The barges tied there were squat and ugly, but me and Loren still came down to watch the boats glide by and say what we would do if we owned any of them. We always came in the day, never at night.

The fence across the pier was in bad condition. In the darkness I could see its ragged silhouette against the neon lights. I had seen men fishing on the pier and had wanted to fish with Loren, but he said that his father told him there were rats all around the pier.

Reuben walked a little way out on the pier and sat down on a wooden piling.

I was so scared. *Oh God, please don't let my father jump in the water.* I was crying and trying to stop from crying at the same time. I was thinking that I should go call Mom or the police, but I was afraid that if I left, I wouldn't see him again. I didn't want to see him go into the water, but I was afraid to leave and not see what he was going to do.

I was shaking and it was getting hard for me to breathe. The rain had stopped and it was getting colder. There was little light behind Reuben, and I could barely see his dark form. I wondered what Mom would do, and I thought she would call to him, or maybe go over to him.

He didn't move for a long time, and I finally stopped crying. I started thinking about Mr. Moses sitting in the church and looking at the man after the lynching. He said the man had not been the same after his friend had been lynched, had stopped being whole, and had died.

I thought the man had just become so sad that he just didn't want to live anymore. I thought that Reuben was that sad now. I could feel his sadness all in me and felt that my whole body was crying. I didn't want to lose him.

It was so cold on the pier.

I thought about the man in the church, and then I thought about him watching as they were about to hang his friend, and I wondered how he felt. Did he feel cold? Did he shake like I was shaking?

I got up and edged my way toward Reuben.

"Go home," he said quietly.

I felt for a place to sit and sat next to him.

"Go home, boy," he said again. This time his voice

was rough, but not mad like it had been before. It was a weary voice, as if he was really exhausted.

"I'm cold," I said.

He didn't answer.

"You think there are rats under the pier?" I asked.

"You scared?" he asked me.

"Yes."

"You a boy or a little girl?" he asked. "You scared of a rat?"

"I'm scared of what's happening," I said. "I don't want to be sitting in the dark. I want to be home with you and Mom and Ty."

"Go on home."

"Come with me."

"I ain't got no home," he said. "Your mama pays the bills—it's her home, not mine."

"Everybody got a home. Just sometimes we're not in them. You and me got a home," I said. "We just need to get in it. We just need to make it okay. We can do that."

"I don't need your advice."

"Would you hold me?"

"Why?"

"I'm cold."

"What you coming out here in the middle of the night for?" he asked. "Walking in the rain without a coat on or . . ."

Silence. Then the sound of the water slapping against

the pier. Cars humming along the highway. I slid closer and leaned against him. I could feel his warmth as I sat next to him. He put his arm around me, and we sat for a while and then I was crying again. At first he didn't say anything and then he asked me why I was crying, and I said I didn't know exactly. He said that was okay, not to know exactly.

The sky turned gray, then it streaked with light over the river, and the outlines of the buildings broke through. Then it was light and there was a new day starting. And it was Reuben standing up and pulling me to my feet, and us walking together.

"Look at us, two bums walking through Harlem. We don't have enough money between us to get a subway ride," he said. "Ain't that a shame?"

"It's okay."

"And what were you going to do if I fell in the river? You going to jump in and pull me out? I bet you don't even know how to swim. Do you?"

"I can swim a little," I said.

"You can't swim good without lessons," Reuben said. "You want to learn how to swim good?"

"Sure."

We got to the block and there was a police car in front of the house. Reuben saw it and stopped.

"It's okay," I said.

He told me to go upstairs and get some money out of his pants so we could go buy some breakfast. I asked him if he was going to wait for me to come back.

"I'll be here," he said.

I don't know why I had to whisper it, but I did. I tiptoed and whispered in his ear. "Daddy, don't leave."

He said he wouldn't.

tHe DReaM

In my dream I was standing on a wooden balcony *in a small town, the kind you see in old cowboy movies. The houses were low and square with wooden shingles. All of them had balconies. There were people standing, as I was, or sitting with their legs dangling over the sides. It was bright out, not sunny, but still bright.*

The wide street below the balconies was empty except for two men. One was tall with wide shoulders that sloped slightly to one side as he walked; the other man was smaller and had an orange-colored backpack. Then I heard a slight rumbling. It sounded like thunder and I looked up at the sky, but it was still clear. People on the balconies were shouting and closing their shutters. Some were pointing down the road. I looked to see what they were pointing at and saw hundreds of tiny things coming toward the middle of town. Even without knowing what they were, I could sense that they were dangerous.

The smaller man began to run as the creatures—I could see that they were rats, but not ordinary rats; they had rat bodies and human faces—were drawing closer. I turned toward the two men and saw that the small man was not a man at all. It was Loren. I screamed for him to run. I watched Loren running toward one of the houses. He banged on a closed door with both fists. It opened for only a second and he rushed inside.

I turned to see what the other man was doing and saw that he had fallen. The rats were screaming as they attacked the man on the ground. They were all around him, biting at him, jumping toward his face and chest, and he was beating them back with his hands. It was my father!

Looking around for a way to get off the balcony to go help him, I saw that there weren't any doors or windows into the building. I tried to climb over the railing, but it just got higher and higher. There was nothing I could do but look down into the street and watch the rats attacking.

My father was still in the street below me, and I was shocked to see what he was doing. The rats were on him and he was fighting them off. It was the same motions he made when he was lying on the bed, except now I could see what he was fighting. And then, as suddenly as they had come, the rats began to speed off. They made an eerie, shrill noise that echoed against the old buildings. In the middle of the *road, fighting frantically as if the rats were still there, was my father.*

Alone on the balcony, I knew I was dreaming, and at the same time I was watching the dream, and it was filling my head with meanings and feelings, and I knew I would wake up with it in my mind.

When I came out of the dream, I was sweating and breathing hard. It was still dark. In the glow of the light from the radio dial I looked at where Ty lay sleeping. The linoleum floor was cool against my feet as I went to my parents' bedroom and eased the door open slightly. Mom's steady breathing was good. I knew that Daddy was at work.

"I never have a dream," Loren said. "I don't even remember going to bed. I get in bed and then—bang!— it's morning."

"That's because you still have a baby brain," I said. "Babies don't dream."

I had told Loren about my dream, but not that I had that same dream, with the rats and my father in the street, over and over again. It came so many times that I didn't want to go to sleep. I wanted to tell my father about my dream, but I thought it wasn't time yet. He had found a job in a warehouse, loading groceries at night for morning deliveries. He slept in the daytime. When he slept, I could hear him talking in his sleep. If I opened his door, I could see his body jerk and move as if he was moving away from something that was after him.

When school was first out and the city streets were taking on the sweaty excitement of summer, I had thought that growing up meant understanding every-thing. But now that I understood more things, yet couldn't change how people lived their lives or how they suffered as they fought their demons, I knew that understanding wasn't enough. I wanted to understand how people lived, and what they were feeling, and I thought I was smart enough, or maybe able to sense what was happening. I just didn't know what I could do with it all, or if I could hold all the feelings inside of me.

The last time I saw Mr. Moses was the day me and Loren and Sessi were sitting on the stoop and he came and said he just needed to say good-bye to us. He had a suitcase with him. It was old, with a strap around the middle, and one end was held together with heavy black tape.

"Why you going?" Loren asked.

"Well, son, old men fly away with their dreams, just disappear into the night," Mr. Moses said. "And young men with vision take their place. It's time for me to take these old bones south where the weather is a lot warmer and a lot kinder."

"Like the birds," Sessi said.

Mr. Moses looked at Sessi and grinned. "Yeah, just like them birds heading home."

I asked him if he was going to take the subway down-town to the train, and when he said yes, I told him I would carry his bag to the station.

"It makes me feel good to see such fine young men like you and Mr. Hart," he said.

"I had a dream, but it wasn't a good one."

Mr. Moses stopped and looked at me. He nodded, and then he started again toward Malcolm X Boulevard. We walked slowly, and I was thinking about telling him my dream. I didn't, but I had the feeling that he might know. I did ask him if he thought that I could change my dreams if I wanted.

"David, we build our dreams deep down in our souls. We use everything we ever knew and everything that's ever touched us," Mr. Moses said. "You've got a strong heart and a strong mind. If this old world can be changed, it'll be because you've nudged it toward the dreams you build. I got faith in you, David. I got a real true faith in you."

At the top of the stairs he took the bag and held out his hand.

"Take care of yourself," I said as we shook hands.

"And you take care of yourself, Mr. David," he answered.

He went down the stairs into the darkness of the station and blended into that darkness. I started to walk away and then stopped. I wanted to ask him how he had known for sure that he was a dream bearer. I ran down the stairs, but a train was just pulling out of the station. I looked around to see if Mr. Moses was still on the platform, but he wasn't.

There were more things I wanted to say to him, and things I wanted to ask him, but he was gone. I was sure I would never see him again. A feeling of sadness washed over me but it didn't last. I knew he would be in my mind for as long as I lived.

Ty said he was going to get serious about his education, but I knew he wasn't sincere. All he wanted to do was to hang out with his friends and live in their little pretend world. His world wasn't any more real than his comic book characters, but somehow he was still believing in it. Mom said the streets could suck your brains out, and I thought that was true. I just wondered how much of Ty's brain would have to be sucked out before he got himself together.

I didn't call my father Reuben anymore after the night we were on the pier together. I realized that somewhere in his life he had lost part of himself and was searching for it. Even in his dreams he was searching for parts that would make him whole.

What I did think was that, for the first time, I was part of his dreaming too. Perhaps when he was alone with his eyes closed, he saw me. Or maybe I could help him build a new one, with the whole family in it with him.

Things had been difficult at the beginning of summer, and in many ways they still were. Nothing wonderful had come into my life to solve all the problems, or even to make them easier to deal with. What I remember most, besides the being scared and the wonder of how things could go so wrong, was the old man. When he had gone, I thought about him sitting on the park bench talking about his dreams. I couldn't touch him anymore, or hear his voice, but his dreams were still with me, were part of me. I had taken the dreams and made them part of who I was, and somehow, because the dreams were about events that happened so long ago, I felt older, stretched back to a different place and time. I still felt afraid when I thought about the man being hung, or about his friend who couldn't move. I know I will always carry those dreams with me. I know my father's dreams will be mine, too.

I think that what people dream, what they take into their minds to hold or worry about or, like Daddy, fight against, is what you have to know to really understand them. And once you know someone like that, once you understand what makes them dream, you can't ever let it go.

Sometimes, when I'm alone, I feel good about the dream I had about Daddy. I don't know everything about him, but I think I know more about what is happening inside of him when he is nervous, when he makes little grunting noises in his sleep and jerks around. When I hear him at night, still fighting in his sleep, I want to go into the room and sit by the bed and tell him that everything will be all right. But then, sometimes, I don't want to know what he is dreaming. It gets me really down thinking about his demons when I know I can't do anything about them. I think that's what Mr. Moses was talking about when he said he wanted to give his dreams to somebody else. He knew he couldn't, and now I knew it, too. Still, there's a part of me that wants to know everything about everybody, no matter how hard it gets.

I decided I didn't want to go all the way up to Riverdale, so me and Loren get to go to school together again. Mom was a little disappointed, but when I told her I didn't want to have to make a whole lot of changes in my life, she understood. I knew she would.

The weather got real hot, and it looked like everything on the block went into slow motion. The superintendent told Sessi that she had to take her house down, and she asked me and Loren to help her.

"My house wasn't bothering anyone," Sessi complained.

The sides of Sessi's little house had turned brown and brittle, and they snapped as she and Loren were taking it down. They were putting the dried sticks and leaves into plastic bags to take downstairs for the garbage. From where I stood, I could see all the rooftops in the neighborhood and the crisscross of streets that stretched toward the hill. The cars and buses looked like toys and the people like tiny fairy-tale creatures scurrying about their business. I thought about Daddy looking down from his roof when he was young, and having picnics with his family. I wondered what all those people down there were thinking about, and what they saw when they closed their eyes.

WALTER DEAN MYERS

is the author of *Monster*, the first winner of the Michael L. Printz Award, a National Book Award Finalist, a Coretta Scott King Honor Book, and a *Boston Globe–Horn Book Honor Book*; *Handbook for Boys*; *Patrol*, illustrated by Ann Grifalconi; *Bad Boy: A Memoir*; *Malcolm X: A Fire Burning Brightly*, illustrated by Leonard Jenkins; the Caldecott Honor Book *Harlem*, illustrated by Christopher Myers; and the Newbery Honor Books *Scorpions* and *Somewhere in the Darkness*. A publishing institute, part of the biannual Langston Hughes Children's Literature Festival, has been established in his name. An ever-popular literary figure, he has been a guest at the White House and has made numerous appearances in conjunction with the National Basketball Association's "Read to Achieve" program. Walter Dean Myers lives in Jersey City, New Jersey, with his family.